THE
SEER OF SHADOWS

MORE BOOKS BY AVI

AVI
THE
SEER OF SHADOWS

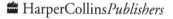

HarperCollins*Publishers*

Library of Congress Cataloging-in-Publication Data

Avi, 1937–
The seer of shadows / by Avi. — 1st ed.
p. cm.
Summary: In New York City in 1872, fourteen-year-old Horace, a
photographer's apprentice, becomes entangled in a plot to create fraudulent
spirit photographs, but when Horace accidentally frees the real ghost of a
dead girl bent on revenge, his life takes a frightening turn.
ISBN 978-0-06-000015-8 (trade bdg.)
ISBN 978-0-06-000016-5 (lib. bdg.)
[1. Photography—History—Fiction. 2. Ghosts—Fiction. 3. Swindlers and
swindling—Fiction. 4. Revenge—Fiction. 5. New York (N.Y.)—History—
1865–1898—Fiction. 6. Horror stories.] I. Title.
PZ7.A953Sf 2008   2007010891
[Fic]—dc22   CIP
                                                                   AC

Typography by David Caplan
5 6 7 8 9 10
❖
First Edition

FOR WALTER DEAN MYERS
SPECIAL THANKS TO ARLENE ROBILLARD,
WHO POINTED THE WAY

ONE

IT WAS AN OCTOBER MORNING in the year 1872, and New York City's air was so befogged with white mist and dark smoke that I could barely see across the street. All the same I was attending to my daily chore of sweeping our small front court with its painted sign:

ENOCH MIDDLEDITCH
SOCIETY PHOTOGRAPHER

Chancing to look up, I was startled to see a black girl standing just beyond our low iron gate. It was as if she had just stepped out of the haze, dressed in her somber cotton servant's garb. A tiny wisp of curly black hair poked out from beneath her white cap. Though clearly she was a servant, her posture was upright, quite proud, and not at all deferential. I judged her to be about the same age as I, fourteen; but her smooth face, round and dark, seemed devoid of emotion until I noticed her eyes: They were full of a deep and brooding intensity.

My first thought was that she was looking at me, but then I realized it was our sign that held her attention.

"May I help you?" I asked.

She turned her gaze upon me. "Who are you?"

The question, asked so bluntly, was unexpected. "I'm Mr. Middleditch's apprentice."

"Does he make portraits?"

"Portraits, *cartes de visite*, and studies."

"My mistress, Mrs. Frederick Von Macht, requires a portrait."

"Then you've come to the right place."

"Good," said the girl. "She will be at your door tomorrow, at two."

Though surprised by her presumption, I said, "I'll tell my employer," perfectly aware that Mr. Middleditch had no pressing matters to attend to. Business was anything but lively.

With a curt nod the girl turned and walked away, vanishing into the mist as eerily as she had appeared.

Not only did I wonder where she'd come from and gone to, I was uncertain whether to believe her or not. But knowing it would be a good thing if her mistress did come for a sitting, I put aside such questions and hurried into our rooms to inform Mr. Middleditch that he actually had a customer.

Still, there was something very unsettling about the girl, so much so that I could not get her out of my mind. Was it the way she'd suddenly appeared and disappeared into the mist? Was it the tone of her voice? Was it the brooding look in her eyes?

That said, I shall be the first to admit there was nothing about her appearance to foretell the extraordinary events that were to follow.

TWO

MY NAME IS HORACE CARPETINE. I was born in New York City and spent my youth there. Perfectly happy years they were, too, though my childhood occurred during the vast upheaval known as the Civil War. And I can assure you there was nothing civil about that conflict, certainly not in New York City.

My father, short, stocky, and bald, was a watch repairer about whom always wafted a faint smell of fine machine oil. An early and fervent supporter of Abolition and radical Republicans, he was devoted to the likes of Abraham Lincoln and New York's Horace Greeley. In fact, it was from Mr. Greeley that my first name was derived.

Father, a great believer in science, considered all superstition bunkum. Every occurrence, he thought, had a rational explanation. All matters should be considered in the light of honest logic. Not surprisingly, I was brought up to think the same.

My mother was a seamstress of fancy frocks working at home for a milliner who dubbed herself Madame D'Arco.

I had an older brother and an even older sister. My sister, Harriet (named after the writer Harriet Beecher Stowe), settled her fortunes by marrying Mr. Toby McClain, a customs house clerk. By the time this story begins, I was already an uncle.

My brother, John (named after John Brown, the martyred Abolitionist), had been taken into my father's watch shop and was destined to make that his life's occupation.

I, much the youngest, was in many respects raised as an only child, living with my parents in a third-floor apartment on Mulberry Street in Manhattan. I was quick to learn, and by the time I approached my fourteenth birthday I was quite verbal, a good reader, and could do sums and geometry. My father enjoyed engaging me in what he called "philosophical arguments," when we would debate such questions as "What is truth?" or "What is more useful in the modern age, logic or faith?"

In fact, Father liked to brag I was a model youth for the industrial age. Had I not won school prizes for mathematics and practical science? Was not one of my heroes John Ericsson, the great, self-taught engineer?

When my schooling was complete, it was necessary to find me a suitable trade. Given my skills and taste, Father decided it should be work of a scientific nature. As it happened, one of his customers learned that a photographer by the name of Enoch Middleditch needed a boy to serve as live-in helper: an apprentice.

In those days, while photographs were to be seen everywhere, it was the rare individual who could explain the process by which they were made. Photography required knowledge of mechanics, physics, and chemistry.

Photographic images were considered remarkably truthful, reality itself. "Paintings may be beautiful," my father argued. "But they are only artists' notions. Photography reveals facts." He would point to the daguerreotype of my grandfather on the wall. "You see," he would say, "that is him!"

Inquiries were made about Mr. Middleditch. "He's a very successful photographer," Father soon informed me. "Quite wealthy."

"How do you know?"

"He told me so himself, and he strikes me as an honest fellow."

Things were soon arranged. In return for being Mr. Middleditch's apprentice, I would have room, board, and, most importantly, instruction in the science of photography.

Upon entering my new life, I took my mother's love, my

father's ideals, and their parting gift of a copy of Dr. J. Towler's book:

THE SILVER SUNBEAM
A PRACTICAL AND THEORETICAL TEXT-BOOK
ON
SUN DRAWING AND
PHOTOGRAPHIC PRINTING
And God said, let there be light: and there was light

When Father presented the volume to me, he assured me that despite the biblical quote on the title page, its three hundred and forty-nine pages contained only rational knowledge.

So it was that on March the first, 1872, I left home and moved in with Mr. Middleditch, resolved to be nothing less than the best photographer in this world.

Other worlds were not mentioned.

THREE

MIDDLEDITCH WAS HIS TRUE NAME. He claimed it was of English derivation. Its singularity, moreover, was something of which he was absurdly pleased. He liked to say that its oddness meant that people would remember it. In the world of photography, ever more crowded with amateurs as well as professionals, he insisted it was vital to be noticed.

He rented the lowest floor in a common brownstone house in the Manhattan district known as Greenwich Village, 40 Charlton Street. The rooms, set low in the house, were gloomy. But when you consider how photographic images were made—in semidarkness—it was actually an advantage.

The front parlor was a reception space for clients. The second room was where he took his photographs. A third room contained his equipment and was where the photographic plates were processed. Chemical smells tinged the air.

Beyond these rooms was a small, private living space, consisting of his bed-sitting room, plus a kitchen of sorts. I slept in the kitchen. Beneath my narrow bed I stored an old sailor's chest in which I kept some personal items, my copy of *The Silver Sunbeam*, and the little bit of money I called my own.

The entry to our quarters was through the front court, where the sign, which proclaimed Mr. Middleditch a "society" photographer, made its appeal to New York snobbery. But once I had established myself in Charlton Street, I discovered that Mr. Middleditch's business did not thrive. He'd greatly exaggerated his wealth and position to my father and struggled to eke out a living. He claimed he did not care, saying he was an *artiste,* even speaking the word with a French accent.

Truth be known, Mr. Middleditch was lazy. Still, he was a good teacher and more than willing to instruct me in the secrets of the photographic art. I'm sure he did so not because of any particular generosity, but because I could do more work while he did less.

In fact, though I did lots of sweeping, dusting, and brushing of jackets, I was taught a very great deal about aperture and shutter speed, the essence of photography. My fingertips soon grew black with photo chemicals, the mark of the true photographer.

In my first few months, things went well. Very soon I was

setting up cameras, adjusting lenses, and preparing photographic plates, both negatives and positives. While I was thus engaged in my regular duties, Mr. Middleditch busily chatted with his occasional clients, "fishing them," as people said.

If there was one thing my employer was good at, it was taking advantage of a situation. Thus, as I readied the photographic wet plates, he, with flourish and fuss, spent time arranging his subjects.

"I wish the world to see how beautiful you are" was his standard phrase for women.

For men it was "Sir, we must capture your sense of dignity and power."

His subjects duly flattered, Mr. Middleditch would duck beneath the black cloth behind the camera box and press the air bulb that powered the shutter release. The image was thus captured. Then he reappeared and chatted some more while I attended to the critical work of developing the photographic glass plate.

I never actually took pictures. Mr. Middleditch insisted upon doing that. It was a point of honor with him and frustration for me. When I asked when I might, he'd say, "In time, Horace, in time."

Such a response only increased my desire to actually take pictures. How could I ever become a photographer unless I tripped the shutter? How little did I guess the result when the opportunity at last arrived!

FOUR

MRS. FREDERICK VON MACHT came to our door promptly at two o' clock. When the knock came, Mr. Middleditch bolted into his workspace to suggest that he was busy, while I went to the door and opened it.

Mrs. Von Macht was a tall, meticulously groomed woman dressed entirely in black. True, in those days black clothing was to be seen everywhere on both men and women. But her silk garments were especially elegant: a high-necked and narrow hourglass over-jacket in the fashionable style of the day, set over a skirt long enough so that her patent leather shoes were all but invisible. Fine black kid gloves concealed her hands. The hat she wore was decorated with dark bird plumes. In one hand she carried a little purse, a reticule of black jet beads.

Her face was quite attractive, with brown eyes that seemed to convey deep sorrow. Her cheeks were pale and smooth, her brow unlined, her mouth as delicately set as a rose, her chin beautifully formed. Her long black hair was pulled back and shaped into a chignon at the nape of her neck. Not a hair was out of place. I could also detect a faint smell of lilac perfume.

In short, my quick judgment proclaimed her the very image of a dignified and attractive woman, a woman in firm control of her world and herself. What's more, she had come in a fine horse and carriage—with a coachman.

Obviously Mrs. Von Macht was wealthy. But the black band around her left arm made it clear that she was also in mourning, if highly fashionable mourning.

Her servant girl was with her. But other than to notice her as the same black girl I'd met previously, I paid her little mind. As far as I was concerned, she was of no consequence to our business with Mrs. Von Macht.

"Yes, madam," I said to the woman. "May I help you?"

"I am Mrs. Frederick Von Macht," the woman replied in a clear but soft voice. "I have an appointment with Mr. Middleditch."

"Yes, madam," I said, making a little bow. "Mr. Middleditch is expecting you."

With a rustle of her heavy skirts, Mrs. Von Macht stepped into our parlor. The servant girl followed.

Our reception room was modest. Two gaslight fixtures on the walls provided soft, pleasant light. This light revealed a small, dark green horsehair sofa and chair. An undersized Turkish rug lay upon the floor while a low table sat before the couch. Upon this table was a portfolio of photographs. Other ornately framed portraits were on the wall.

I need to say that Mr. Middleditch did not take any of these photographs, although this was not something he revealed to his clients.

"Please sit down," I said. "I'll fetch Mr. Middleditch. He's working on some photo plates."

Not true, but it's what I'd been instructed to say.

"Thank you," said the woman, seating herself and taking in the room with a glance, folding her small, delicate hands demurely in her lap. The servant girl, eyes cast down, stood by her side.

I hastened to the studio room. Mr. Middleditch was standing before a looking glass fussing over his neck cloth. Perfection achieved, he slicked down his hair with brilliantine and then smoothed his waxed mustache, of which he was very proud.

Of middling height, Mr. Middleditch was quite stocky: thick arms, large hands, barrel chest. Longish golden hair was brushed back over his collar. His face was as round as a ball, a ball upon which features—wide-set eyes, round nose, and puckered lips—seem to have been affixed with horse glue. His full handlebar mustache was, I will allow, dashing. He did not walk so much as swagger. At the moment he was wearing his best dark four-button cutaway jacket with finely checked trousers and polished boots.

"Mrs. Von Macht is here," I announced.

"What's she like?" he whispered.

I described her, adding, "She's in mourning."

"Perfect!"

"Why?"

"Horace, a pretty woman in mourning gives me emotions on which I can play. Do you think her rich?"

"She came in her own carriage. With a servant."

"Rich, pretty, and in mourning. More than perfect!"

My expression must have shown some objection to such sentiments, for he said, "Horace, we need money."

With a mischievous wink, he added, "Bid me good fishing," and stepped into the front room. I followed and, though I kept my distance, I observed all that transpired.

Mr. Middleditch approached the woman with great deference: body not quiet erect, hands clasped before him— rather, I thought, like an undertaker.

"Mrs. Von Macht," he murmured, "I am Mr. Middleditch—the photographer. Thank you so very much for gracing my parlor. I am at your service, completely." He made a slight bow.

She gazed upon him with cool, appraising eyes.

Apparently satisfied with what she saw, she said, "Mr. Middleditch, I am pleased to meet you. Please sit." She spoke with the air of someone used to giving commands.

Mr. Middleditch dutifully sat and leaned forward slightly. "Madam," he began, "how can I be of service?"

"Mr. Middleditch," said the woman, speaking in a trembling tone, as if raw emotions were just below the surface of a determinedly dignified composure, "I have a request which may appear somewhat odd, but it is, nonetheless, a heartfelt application."

"I assure you, madam, I am pleased merely to have the opportunity to gratify your needs."

Mrs. Von Macht took a deep breath, as if gathering courage to speak. "Last May," she began, "my daughter—Eleanora was her name, and she was only thirteen years of age—passed . . . on." Her voice seemed to quiver.

"I am so very sorry," murmured Mr. Middleditch.

"Scarlet fever," continued Mrs. Von Macht when she recovered her composure. "Quite sudden. And tragic. Eleanora was a charming, lovely . . . fair-haired girl. I loved her very much. As did her father. The truth is, Mr. Middleditch, Eleanora was an angel in life as she must be . . . in death."

As Mrs. Von Macht spoke, the servant shifted slightly, causing me to glance at her. To my great surprise, the girl was shaking her head slightly, as if inwardly contradicting what the woman said. Next moment the girl, realizing I was gazing at her, looked down.

"With such a mother," murmured Mr. Middleditch, who had noticed nothing of the girl's behavior, "I can have little doubt."

"We buried her," the woman continued, "in the family tomb. Brooklyn's Green-Wood Cemetery."

"A beautiful place."

The woman paused and shut her eyes briefly, as if to control the painful memory. After a deep breath, she looked up. "Mr. Middleditch, do you believe in an afterlife?"

Mr. Middleditch, taken by surprise, actually stammered. "Why, I certainly consider myself a . . . a religious man. . . ." His words drifted off inconclusively. (After being with him for some months, I had never noticed his attendance at any church—not once.)

"No," she said softly, her eyes wide and welling with tears. "I mean, do you believe in . . . ghosts?"

FIVE

Mr. Middleditch was at a momentary loss for a reply. I too was startled. "I . . . confess," he managed to stammer, "I've had no . . . personal contact with . . . spirits."

Mrs. Von Macht found a lacy, black-edged handkerchief in her reticule and carefully daubed her eyes before continuing. "Mr. Middleditch," she confided, "I readily acknowledge that I am uncertain about such deep matters. Yet . . . yet if it is true . . . why then—" Her eyes grew teary. She seemed unable to speak.

"It has been suggested to me," she went on when she recovered, "that souls, or ghosts, what some now call the ectoplasm of the departed, linger where they have been laid to rest. I have a feeling"—she put a hand to her heart—"that my daughter, Eleanora, is restless." These last words she all but whispered.

The room was silent for a moment, as if we were all listening for movement from elsewhere.

"How do I know this?" she continued softly. "A mother's heart knows.

"Mr. Middleditch," she continued in a stronger voice, "I have decided that you must make a pleasing photograph of me, which I will frame suitably and affix to Eleanora's tomb. Then, if it is true—if her spirit lingers in melancholy sorrow, missing her grieving mother—why, then, she might see me and thus gain, in her infinite solitude, some comfort."

Hearing Mrs. Von Macht speak, I had no doubt that the woman was talking of her own loneliness and grief.

I suspect Mr. Middleditch observed the same. "Madam," he said, "I fully grasp your perfectly reasonable request. Indeed, I am moved. It's a commission which shall give me honor to fulfill."

"After all," the woman went on, as if feeling the need to justify her request, "I have painted images of her about my house. They comfort me. Why shouldn't I do the same for poor Eleanora? Now that she has died," she added with what I considered an odd afterthought.

"Of course," said Mr. Middleditch, and then, shifting slightly, he looked at me and winked.

For her part Mrs. Von Macht sat there as if lost in her own

grief. That was when the servant girl leaned forward and whispered something into her ear. The woman nodded.

"I have been reminded," said the woman, "of another request. I wish the photograph to be taken in my own rooms. It is to be hoped," she added, "if my surroundings are familiar to Eleanora, it will bring her that much more comfort."

"A kind thought," agreed Mr. Middleditch. "I would like to oblige. However, the art of photography being what it is, the photographic plates have to be processed and used when wet. This is why most of my photographic images are made here, in my studio."

"Could you not set up a temporary studio in my home?" asked the woman. "I should be much obliged."

"I fear water is required."

"I have a scullery with running water which could be placed at your disposal."

"Perfect!"

"Then we have an understanding?" asked the woman.

Mr. Middleditch considered. Then, gently, he said, "I'm afraid your requests add to the expense."

"Cost," replied the woman, "is not a concern."

"Very good," Mr. Middleditch said quickly. "In that case we shall need a two-day appointment, one for establishing a studio in your home and preparing the photographic plates. The second appointment will be used for taking the photographs."

"That will be fine," Mrs. Von Macht assured him.

In deference to the sad feelings aroused, both she and Mr. Middleditch observed a moment of silence.

Then, to my surprise, Mr. Middleditch said, "I suspect your daughter must have been a beautiful young lady. Do you, perchance, have an image of her with you?"

"Not with me," said Mrs. Von Macht, blushing slightly with what I assumed was the fullness of her emotions. "But as I said, there are many in my home."

"Of course!"

A date and hour to take the photographic portrait was set—one week from that day—and a Fifth Avenue address provided. Moreover, Mrs. Von Macht promised to send her carriage round the day before to facilitate the transport of our apparatus.

Agreement reached, Mrs. Von Macht stood up.

Mr. Middleditch hastened to stand and with many thanks and many bows, promised that he and his assistant would be there promptly.

The woman turned to her servant. "Come along, Pegg."

But before the woman could leave Mr. Middleditch said, "Mrs. Von Macht, may I ask how you found me?"

The woman turned with a full swirl of her dress. "Mr. Middleditch," she said sweetly and with a flirtatious blinking of her eyes, "surely you are aware of your very high reputation."

I glanced at the servant girl. Once again I caught her slightly shaking her head.

Mr. Middleditch, however, only glowed with pleasure at the woman's words, thanked her kindly, and followed closely to hand her into the carriage.

I remained behind, as did the servant girl. I wanted to ask her what her head-shaking meant, yet didn't know where to begin. But as the girl started out the door, she abruptly turned about—as if having read my mind—looked fiercely at me, and said, "That is not how Eleanora died! And we're here because Madam wanted an unknown photographer. I found you by walking the streets and seeing your sign!"

I was taken aback, but before I could respond, the girl fled the house.

SIX

I WAS STILL TRYING to make sense of what the girl, Pegg, had said, not even certain I'd heard correctly, when Mr. Middleditch returned to the parlor. All smiles, he was actually rubbing his pudgy hands together.

"Well, Horace," he said gleefully, "what do you make of that?"

"I'm not sure," I said, trying to sort out what had happened. "It's a sad story."

"No doubt," he agreed. "Absolutely. But don't fret. I think I can profit greatly from it." He flung himself on the sofa, fully extended his legs, and put his arms behind his head—all the while grinning broadly.

"Profit, sir?" I said.

"Business lesson number one, Horace! There's no room for sentiment."

"You mean a good portrait shows a person as they really are. The scientific way."

"Oh, piffle. Something more."

"More, sir?"

He sat up, leaned forward, and said, "Horace, didn't you see that woman's clothing? Her carriage? Her address?"

"She's wealthy."

"Exactly! With one of the richest addresses in the city. I suspect she's very rich, Horace. With a name which suggests one of the Old Dutch families. They still have money, you know. As for Green-Wood Cemetery, where her daughter . . . what's her name . . . ?"

"Eleanora."

". . . is buried, nothing could be better. Just the other day the *Times* was saying, to be fashionable, you must live on Fifth Avenue, be seen in Central Park, and be buried in Green-Wood Cemetery." He laughed. "Consider, too, that Mrs. Von Macht came to me because of my very high reputation."

My thoughts went to what the servant girl claimed, that she found my master because Madam wanted "an unknown photographer."

"But, sir, the girl told me that—"

He cut me off with a wave of his hand. "Horace, I'm not interested in a servant's opinions. I need to think how to take best advantage of this situation." With that he jumped up, and brimming with energy—unusual for him—he bolted from our rooms.

I went about my business, which was dusting our rooms and checking to see that various photographic chemicals were in good supply, camera apparatus clean, and lenses free of oily smudges. I hoped that doing these mundane tasks would calm me, for I could not get Mrs. Von Macht's unsettling words—nor the girl's—out of my head.

What troubled me was this: Since nothingness is not a notion that is easily accommodated by a young person's mind, children often believe there is no complete departure from life. Therefore, a child raised with superstition readily accepts the existence of lingering spirits or, in other words, ghosts.

Not me, of course. In my home we considered such beliefs fairy tales. "Let the dead bury the dead" was something my father said often. He meant it in jest. But he also taught me that as long as no harm was being done, it was polite to tolerate such ignorance.

Here, however, I was confronted with the notion of ghosts as believed by an adult. That made me uneasy. Mr. Middleditch's response that, to quote him, he would "greatly profit" from the woman's grief made me even more uncomfortable.

Finally there were the servant's words: "That is not how Eleanora died!" Had I heard correctly?

When Mr. Middleditch returned, he took me to dinner

at O'Tooly's Oyster and Chop House on lower Broadway. O'Tooly's was not a place he frequented, for, though only a few cuts above a rum hole, it was expensive. On those rare occasions when Mr. Middleditch went, I usually was not invited.

That night O'Tooly's was crowded with gentlemen, with a few ladies in attendance. The men, canes or walking sticks in one hand, tankard or shot glass in the other, wore dark suits with buttoned waistcoats along with bowler or top hats. Some had spats on their shoes. Ladies wore long dresses, hats, cheap lace, and jewelry.

Sawdust was on the floor, mirrors shone from the walls, layers of cigar smoke drifted through the air, and the stink of beer, rum, and whiskey irritated my nose. Loud talk and laughter filled my ears: a constant babble of business, politics, women, and horses—in no particular order or interest to me.

After finding us a corner booth, Mr. Middleditch tucked a large white napkin into his collar, ordered drink and oysters for himself, a chop and cider for me.

At first his talk was about New York politics, the doings of Tammany Democrats whom he admired for their ability to manipulate the "riff-raff," and the radical Republicans whom he despised for their belief in social equality. Then the conversation shifted.

"Now then, young Horace Carpetine," he began as he

dried his mustache with his napkin, "when your esteemed father arranged that you be my apprentice, it was so that I might teach you what are known as the tricks of the trade. Very well; we are about to create a major trick."

"Trick, sir?" I said. To me the word suggested dishonesty or even deception.

"Mrs. Von Macht is a grieving mother," Mr. Middleditch went on. "It truly touches my heart." He laid a hand on his waistcoat as if to prove he had one. "I assure you, Horace, it truly does. But I think we can use it to our advantage."

"What do you mean, sir?"

"Horace, the lady desires a photographic portrait to be placed on her beloved daughter's tomb. Well and good! Spiritualism is quite the rage these days. It's as if the war dead have come back to haunt us. A woman like Mrs. Von Macht doesn't want to appear lacking in fashion or sentiment. Society—her kind of society—demands it. What of it? Not so long ago people desired bells attached to the hands of the buried in case they had not died, that they might summon help if prematurely buried. No doubt profitable for bell-makers. No objections from me.

"Business lesson two: In your customers' folly there is profit.

"Very well," he went on, "Mrs. Von Macht further wishes the photograph taken in her own rooms. Horace, I went to look at that home of hers. Very large. Nothing could be better. Why? Because, Horace, I distinctly heard the woman say she had painted images of her daughter all about her house. You heard her, didn't you?"

"Yes," I said, not following his drift.

"Now," he continued, "the lady has made it clear that she believes in spirits. How can we put all this together?"

"I'm sure I don't know, sir."

"Business lesson three: Be inventive." Mr. Middleditch sucked down two sopping wet oysters with considerable gusto, wiped his lips, chin, and mustache dry with his much-spotted napkin, cleared his throat, and said, "We shall provide Mrs. Von Macht with her photograph. But Horace, this photograph shall not only be of her, but also of her dear departed girl, or should I say . . . what's her name?"

"Eleanora."

"Her dear Eleanora's ghost."

"Ghost?" I said, taken by surprise.

"Exactly. I shall make a photograph of that woman, and in that photo there shall also be an image of her daughter—a ghostly image."

"But . . . sir, there are no such things as . . . ghosts."

"Horace, you're either dense or a stiff Puritan! Of course ghosts don't exist. All nonsense and superstition," he said with an authority worthy of my father. "I know that. But"—he wagged a pudgy finger at me—"with the magic of photography I shall *create* a ghost." He grinned with self-delight.

"And she will believe it!"

"But Mr. Middleditch, sir!" I cried. "That would be a terrible thing to do!"

"Well, I don't know," he said, pouting. "I intend to make my fortune with just such items."

"But . . ."

He leaned over the table. "And you, Horace Carpetine, shall have a large part in making it happen. A major part. Naturally you shall share in the rewards, too. Now, eat your chop. I must think it through."

"But—"

"Horace, attend to your food!"

I looked at him and his fat, smiling face. Though full of discomfort, I did as I was bid.

SEVEN

OVER THE NEXT FEW DAYS Mr. Middleditch busied himself with his photographic apparatus with far more energy than usual, but took no time to explain matters further. So it was not until the day before our appointment with Mrs. Von Macht that I learned his plan.

"All right, Master Horace," he said to me that afternoon, "be a good fellow and sit down."

He stood before me in the front parlor, a carpet bag at his feet, fairly well rocking back on his heels so that I had to look up at his burly frame and face.

"Horace," he began, hardly able to suppress a grin, "please attend to me very carefully."

"I always try to do so, sir."

"You've been after me to allow you to do some picture

taking. I am about to give you the opportunity."

"Oh, thank you, sir!" I said with such eagerness that he now laughed aloud.

"Good!" he continued. "Pay close attention."

He reached into his carpet bag and pulled out a cloth package, which he unwrapped with care. Inside was a round, flat, brass object about the diameter of a large apple, not more than an inch thick. A leather thong was attached to either side. The face of this object was smooth, save for what looked like a black button in its middle, and above that, a small, protruding tube. On its perimeter was affixed a little brass plate that gave the name and address of the merchant from whom it had been purchased.

Mr. Middleditch held this thing up with such pride and care that it was clear I was supposed to admire it. But all I could say was "What is it?"

"This, Horace, is the Stirn Concealed Vest Camera. German made. Took a while to track it down. Expensive, too."

"Is it really a camera?"

"This"—he touched the protruding tube—"is the lens, small enough to fit through a buttonhole of your jacket or coat. This"—he touched the central black button—"advances a circular glass photo plate. Each plate allows for six exposures. Here, on the side, is the lever that works the shutter. It's designed to be concealed beneath a coat, jacket, or waistcoat."

"But why would we even use such a thing?"

With a triumphant grin he said, "To take photographs—secretly."

"Secretly, sir?"

"Horace," he cried, "sometimes I forget how young you are. Don't you recall that I said we would be providing Mrs. Von Macht a ghost photograph?"

"I do, sir. But I was hoping you were not . . ."

"Not what?"

Not having the courage to say I thought he was considering something dishonest, I only mumbled, "I thought that you were . . . just joking."

"I assure you, I'm deadly serious." He laughed at his jest. "Now then, pay attention. When we go to the lady's house, while I am taking her portrait, you will—" He stopped, then began again. "Do you remember her saying there are many images of her daughter about the house?"

"Yes, sir."

He placed the thong around my neck so that the spy camera hung upon my chest. "You shall use this camera to take photographs of those portraits of the girl—secretly. By combining my photographic portraits of Mrs. Von Macht with your secret photographs of her daughter's portraits, I shall fashion—with a double exposure—a very fine ghost picture. Or, since I wish to make it high sounding—a spirit image."

He didn't have face enough to contain his smirk.

"Won't she guess?"

"Horace, you know how little people understand the methods by which photographs are made."

Perhaps my look, mirroring my thoughts, brought him a flicker of unease. "Look here, Horace, I promise I'll not *force* Mrs. Von Macht to make any judgments about what she sees. She, for such is her profound sorrow, will come to conclusions entirely on her own. Anyway, this sort of thing works better that way."

The more he laid out the plot, the more my discomfort grew, until I finally blurted, "But . . . why should you even do it?"

"Because my image will provide her with great comfort. She'll believe her departed daughter is well and hovering close. Nothing wrong in that, is there?"

"But it's not—"

"Horace! Is that so very different from what her upstanding minister urges her to believe? Of course, it may well be that Mrs. Von Macht will entertain the notion of more such photos being taken and be willing to pay a handsome price for them. That," he said with a grin, "shall also be her choice. But my profit."

"But sir, won't there be some risk?"

"Risk?"

"What if they discover what I'm doing? You know, taking

". . . those . . . secret pictures?"

"Nothing to worry about," he said, then added, "if you are careful."

Careful! My mind was full of such doubts, questions, and worries it amounted to alarm. But what was I to say? After all, Mr. Middleditch was an adult. My employer. I was apprenticed to him!

"Consider this, too," Mr. Middleditch rushed on with cheerful enthusiasm, "that Mr. Von Macht—as I have taken pains to discover—is a fish merchant. One of the big ones. Thereby, rich. No doubt Mrs. Von Macht has wealthy friends who have their own dear departed. I'll combine being a society photographer with being a . . . spirit photographer." He laughed. "Doesn't that sound fine? Me! A society spirit photographer! Can't you just see it?"

"Yes, sir, I can," I said sulkily.

"Now, Horace," he said, responding to my tone of displeasure, "how many times have you begged me to let you be the photographer? I'm about to give you your chance. Wouldn't you like that?"

"Yes, sir," I muttered. "I would."

"Besides," he said with abrupt sternness, "as my apprentice, it's not for you to question my orders, but to carry them out. Is that understood?"

"Yes, sir," I repeated.

"Very good," said Mr. Middleditch. "Then we must

practice using the concealed camera."

I noted he said *we*, when in fact it was I who would be taking the risk by using his spy camera. But I felt I had little choice in the matter.

That evening, as I lay upon my bed, I went over what Mr. Middleditch was going to do—and my part in it. The sum of it was, he was going to present Mrs. Von Macht with a photograph of such making that she would think the ghost of her daughter was near—seeing something which did not exist!

It was a lie. A hoax. And a cruel one. For all I knew, it was even criminal. What's more, I was being required to have a key part in the misdeed.

I did consider walking away. But where would I go? Not home. I could not expect my parents to take care of me. I was fourteen, old enough to stand on my own. And if I left my apprenticeship, might I not be throwing away my chance of becoming a photographer?

Then, too, was I not going to have a camera in my hands at last? Did I not long to be a photographer? That meant I must take photographs! Should I cast off my first opportunity?

I wondered if I should aim the secret camera the wrong way and thereby spoil his plan. What would that gain me? I might be dismissed outright. I had no doubt Mr. Middleditch could find another boy to get the images he wanted.

In the end I allowed myself to recall my master's words: "I promise I'll not force Mrs. Von Macht to make any judgments about what she sees." With some luck, Mrs. Von Macht would see through the fraud. No harm would be done.

In short I had two hopes: one, no one would be tricked into believing ghosts existed, and two, the fraudulent scheme would not touch me in any way.

As it turned out, both hopes were to be completely dashed.

EIGHT

THE PHOTOGRAPHING of Mrs. Von Macht was set for Saturday. As prearranged, on Friday afternoon she sent her carriage to our door. As soon as we loaded the necessary equipment for our temporary darkroom—we would bring the bulky camera and tripod the next day—the fine horse stepped out smartly, if slowly. A good thing too, since the plate-glass negatives and bottled chemicals were fragile, and the streets with their granite cobblestones were bumpy.

The Von Machts' home was on wide, wealthy, fashionable Fifth Avenue, just above Twenty-seventh Street, north of Madison Square. While more modest than the vast mansions of the Astors and Mr. Vanderbilt, these were elegant homes, quite beyond the apartment dwellings of our downtown neighborhood.

Here, the street was lined with poplar trees, elegant gas lamps, flagstone pavements, and in front of most houses, handsome cast-iron fences. These wealthy homes—three to five stories tall, three windows wide—all had steps (or stoops, as they called them in Dutch New York—and still do) that led up to the first floor's main entrance. Virtually all the houses were faced with brown stone. Well dressed strollers passed by, men in hats, ladies in wide skirts with bustles and bonnets, many with parasols, plus a few nurse-maids with children in tow or in perambulators. No doubt it was the police who made sure there were no common beggars, newsboys, or bootblacks loitering about. Certainly there was less horse manure on the street than elsewhere in the city.

Though Fifth Avenue was crowded with a great variety of fine horse-drawn carriages, wagons, omnibuses, and cabs, we arrived in good time. Of course, as a self-proclaimed *artiste*, Mr. Middleditch was not one to use the servants' entry, commonly found beneath the stoop. So, while I unloaded the plates and chemicals and other apparatus, he went up the steps and worked the bell-pull.

Mrs. Von Macht's servant, Pegg, opened the door, a large door key in hand. Her attentions were all directed at Mr. Middleditch. In fact, I sensed she avoided looking at me. In any case, she carefully set the key down on a little side table by the door, then led us inside.

We went down a long, high, dimly lit hallway. It felt close and thick, akin to the air just before a heavy August storm.

That it was the home of very wealthy people there was no doubt. The floors were richly carpeted. The ceiling, from which hung an unlit gas chandelier, was decorated with elaborate plaster cornices, painted in three tones so as to accentuate richness. The walls were covered over by French paper of a deep red color. As an added touch there were candled wall sconces, though at the moment only one candle was lit.

We passed two paintings on a wall. One was of a dignified man in a military uniform—perhaps from the Mexican War. The other picture was of a girl. The girl's portrait was draped with black cloth, so I assumed it was a painting of Mrs. Von Macht's deceased daughter, Eleanora. I gazed up at her.

As painted, the long hair was light, the face pale, the eyes clear, and the frock a pure white. There was a delicate mouth, too, with a touch of dimple on one cheek. But while everything helped confirm my impression that the girl must have been the sweet angel her mother described, there was a lurking hint of some other complex emotion or tension which I could not identify. Unfortunately, I passed too quickly to take in more.

As for Mr. Middleditch, he barely noticed the painting other than to say, "Lovely girl," while adding his bothersome wink. It was a clear message that this must be one of the paintings I should photograph. My response was renewed guilt as to the swindle we were about to enact, as well as nervousness concerning my part in it.

Farther along the hall we passed a wide flight of steps that led upward. At the foot of these steps stood a grandfather clock ticking with a monotony that suggested time was of no import. On the other side of the hall were large, closed double doors, so I could not see into that room, not then.

Upon reaching the far end of the hall, Pegg led us down a narrow flight of steps. This brought us to the lower floor and a hall, also narrow.

"The coal storage is in the back," said the girl. "The scullery is up front." It proved to be a small room with half windows that made the light dim. I could make out a water tap, a long marble table, tile floors with drains, and some large zinc tubs with scrub boards and a mangle off to one side. It smelled of soap.

"Excellent," proclaimed Mr. Middleditch, whose barely suppressed grin told me he was enjoying himself immensely. "Now if you will take me to Mrs. Von Macht, my boy will set things up."

The girl curtsyed. "This way, please."

When they were gone, I set to work by nailing yellow paper over the small windows. That gave us the dim light and hue required for the manipulation of the photographic plates. Other colors or too much brightness would cause the plates to turn black from overexposure.

The diffused light obtained, I brought out the bottled chemicals and, as was my habit, lined them up in order of use. Then I set out the plate vises, drying racks, and suction-cup devices that allowed me to avoid touching the photographic plates with my fingers—grease and dust being the great enemies of photography, particularly in New York City, where grime is everywhere.

Finally I began to prepare the glass plates—each six and a half inches by four and a half inches—upon which the negative images would be created.

I began by cleaning the glass with a mixture of bichromate of potash, sulfuric acid, and water. As always it stank and made my nose itch.

After using cotton swabs to dry the glass, I wrapped the plates loosely in paper to keep out dust and laid them in a row on the marble table. No sooner had I done that, there was a knock on the door. I thought it might be Mr. Middleditch. It was the servant girl.

"Mr. Middleditch is with my mistress," she said. "Is there anything I can do for you?"

"No, thank you."

To my surprise she did not leave but remained and gazed upon my work with open curiosity. For my part I was not above taking kindly to her interest and presumed admiration. My parents taught me that intolerance was despicable, that I should be open and friendly to all kinds of people. Then too, the better I got on with the girl, the more easily I'd be able to ask about those odd comments she'd made when she'd left our rooms.

So I said, "Stay if you like, but you must close the door. I can't have light."

She did as I bid.

After observing me for a while, she said, "What are you doing?"

Trying to sound professional, I said, "I am about to prepare the materials for making the negative plate."

I held up a glass bottle, which had been painted black. "In our studio I mixed two ounces nitrate of silver with twenty-five ounces of water. It's the nitrate of silver that makes the image. When exposed to light, the silver specks get darker. Do you see my fingers?"

I showed her my black-stained hands. "Photographer's hands," I informed her with pride.

She nodded solemnly.

"Then I added three grains of iodide of potassium."

"What does that do?"

"I don't know," I admitted, blushing to have my self-importance so easily pricked.

Thankfully, she did not laugh, and the exchange had the effect of putting us on a more equal footing.

Still talking as I worked, I said, "I'll take up a glass plate—

using the suction cup to avoid touching it—and pour some collodion and—"

"What's . . . collodion?"

"Like thin glue. It holds the silver nitrate in place. See, I pour the collodion on the glass. Now I tip the glass this way and that so that the collodion covers it evenly. Takes a while to set. You want it tacky so as to hold the silver nitrate."

There I hesitated. I also needed to treat the circular glass plate for my secret camera. I glanced at the girl and decided she had no full idea what I was doing and would react to my round glass in just the same way as she did the regular plates.

So it happened. If she noticed anything out of the ordinary, she said not a word.

I continued: "Over the plates—lightly—I put some paper, to keep away the dust. Now, I'm setting a little tab on each paper. Not that I expect anyone to move them, but if there's some shaking, or wind, the plates might gather dust. A shift of the tab will tell me if that has happened."

The girl nodded.

"And that's all I'll do today. The rest is for tomorrow, when we take the photographs."

"Will you take them?" she asked.

"Mr. Middleditch will take the photos of Mrs. Von Macht," I said, not about to admit what I'd be doing. "Will you take me to him?"

"Yes, sir. Of course."

"You don't need to call me sir."

"As you wish."

I looked around. "Can we make sure no one comes here?" I asked.

"Mrs. Von Macht says while you are here it's to be your room." From her apron pocket she took out a small key. "No one will enter."

"Good."

She locked the room and gave me the key. I put it in my pocket.

As we started up the steps, it occurred to me that I should scout out the pictures of the daughter so that things might go better—which is to say, faster—for me the next day. It was also an opportunity to question the girl about her remarks from the other day. "Did you know Mrs. Von Macht's daughter?" I asked.

"I did."

"Is that her in the painting in the hall upstairs?"

"It is."

"What was she like?" I asked.

She hesitated before replying. "She was my mistress's daughter."

Upon reaching the top of the steps, I paused. "What did you think of her?"

"A girl in my position is not expected to have thoughts about such things," she said. I noticed that her hands had become balled into fists; my question had made her tense.

"Then why," I said, thinking I had cleverly trapped her, "did you tell me that the girl did not die of a fever? You did say that, didn't you?"

Frowning, Pegg hastened down the hallway, as if to get away.

I called after her. "You didn't like her, did you?"

It was as if she had been stung. She whirled about and cried, "I loved Eleanora! As she loved me! No two sisters were ever closer!" I was too startled to respond. In any case she turned away, as if huffed that I'd tricked her into saying too much.

Not knowing what else to do, I went closer to the portrait and gazed upon it. As I'd first observed, Eleanora Von Macht had a sweet face. And yet . . . as I'd noticed before, the painter had caught something else: a certain look about the eyes—or was it the mouth?—which I could not quite grasp. Some sadness or . . . was it anger . . . ?

"Is this a good likeness?" I said.

"Somewhat," the servant girl whispered.

I shifted slightly so I could see Pegg. She was staring up at the painting, as if speaking to it rather than to me.

"Are there other pictures of her about the house?" I asked in as casual a way as I could.

"No."

Taken by surprise, I blurted out, "Your mistress said otherwise."

"She lied," Pegg snapped. Then she immediately edged down the hallway as if regretting having spoken.

My thoughts shifted between working out how I should position myself to photograph the painting and trying to grasp what Pegg was saying. How could I get her to speak and reveal more?

I gazed up at the painting again. As I did, I became aware that Pegg had crept back and was standing directly behind me. She was breathing deeply, as if agitated by some great emotion. The next moment I heard her whisper, "Madam was very cruel to Eleanora."

"What?" I whispered, uncertain if I'd heard right.

"Eleanora died . . . because . . . because the Von Machts neglected her greatly."

"How neglected?" I said, having the presence of mind not to look about.

"They said she'd disobeyed them, and then, as punishment, they kept her isolated and weak. When she fell into a decline, they would not send for the doctor."

"But . . . why would they do that to their daughter?"

"She was not their daughter."

"Then, who—?"

One of the hall doors opened, and Mr. Middleditch stepped out from the room. He bowed to someone inside. "Until tomorrow, madam," he said, shutting the door. Turning about, he saw me. "Ah, Horace, there you are. Are the plates all ready?"

"Yes, sir."

"Dust-free? Secure?"

I patted the key in my pocket. "Yes, sir."

"Good lad," he said. He nodded to Pegg. "We shall return tomorrow."

The girl led us down the hall. As we went, I glanced back, wanting to get another look at Eleanora's portrait.

"Horace!" called Mr. Middleditch. "Come along!"

I swung about. Pegg was glaring at me fiercely.

As we stepped out into the bright autumn sunlight, Pegg slammed the door behind us, rather more forcibly than necessary. I thought, *Something is very wrong.*

NINE

PEGG'S WORDS SO TROUBLED ME that over dinner I told Mr. Middleditch what she had said about the Von Machts' daughter: that Eleanora wasn't their daughter, that they treated her cruelly, that she hadn't died of a fever.

"Now, Horace," said Mr. Middleditch, leaning over his boiled beef and pointing his fork toward me as if to pierce me with his judgment, "who should you believe? The elegant, wealthy Mrs. Von Macht or an ignorant black girl?"

"But Mr. Middle—"

"Horace, I do hope your father isn't one of those radical Republicans. One of those who thinks blacks should be educated or—what are they proposing now?—even vote! Oh, goodness! You're not named after that awful radical Horace Greeley, are you?"

Before I could answer, he waved a hand. "Never mind. Look here, Horace, a black servant girl is bound to be fanciful about another girl who—being about the same age and white—was naturally set over her. The servant probably fancies herself the daughter now. Jealousy, Horace, jealousy. I'll even wager the girl's touched." He tapped his head. "Let me teach you something, Horace. America calls itself a democracy. I'm all for it. Trouble is, the ignorant sometimes think it applies to them."

"But—"

"Eat your food, Horace, and let adults provide you with the proper answers to weighty questions."

I bowed over my food, too cowed to object. But after a while I said, "Sir, when I'm taking my pictures, what should I say if someone finds me in a forbidden place in the Von Macht house?"

He laughed. "Just say you are going about admiring it."

"They won't think me a sneak thief, will they?"

He grinned. "Are you?"

"No!"

"Well, then . . ."

I spent a restless night, tense about the fraud we were about to put into effect. What if I were discovered? What if I did poorly? I kept thinking, too, about Mrs. Von Macht. With the painted image of that angelic girl in my mind, I tried to understand how the sorrowful mother must feel.

That we were taking advantage of her irrational beliefs added to my discomfort.

Then there was Pegg and her words. A complete contradiction! She did act strange. But the cruel notions Mr. Middleditch expressed were so counter to the ideals my family taught me that I preferred to believe Pegg. The truth was, I was beginning to really dislike Mr. Middleditch. Yet if Pegg spoke true . . . what did it mean?

In the end I put my thoughts to the fact that I was about to take my first pictures. There, at last, was something good.

But my unease would not leave me.

TEN

THE NEXT AFTERNOON—Saturday—proved pleasantly
cool: another beautiful autumn day, air fresh and
bright, the city stench and smoke in retreat, Fifth Avenue
trees primed with orange, yellow, and red. True, all would
soon be brittle and gray—more dust added to the city's
grime—but New York City's beauty was there for the seeing.

From somewhere Mr. Middleditch had secured an over-
coat that he instructed me to wear. Purposefully large, it was
meant to conceal the camera which hung around my neck.
As we jogged along in Mrs. Von Macht's carriage, the camera kept banging my chest, an annoying reminder of my
unpleasant task.

Mr. Middleditch, sensing my edginess, patted me on the
knee while whispering into my ear, "You want to help Mrs.

Von Macht become happier, don't you?"

"Yes, sir."

"Do your task and she will."

"With a trick for the gullible?" I muttered.

He laughed. "All life is a trick." Then, with a nod toward the carriage driver and a finger to his lips, he shook his head by way of warning.

I dared say no more.

Arriving, we hauled up Mr. Middleditch's camera. As I labored, my secret camera kept bumping, bumping.

Pegg, as before, let us in. "Madam is expecting you," she said.

Once again I sensed she was avoiding looking at me.

I followed Mr. Middleditch into the front parlor. The soft light from a candelabrum cast a warm glow over the whole room. Thick curtains were pulled over the tall front windows so as to bar any outside light. A small fire was smoldering, making the room overly warm—and me in that coat.

Walls were papered lavishly, covered by an array of pictures, chromo prints, Currier and Ives lithographs, silhouettes, and mirrors, all elaborately framed. But I saw not one image of the girl, a reminder that Pegg might have spoken true.

There were a few stuffed chairs, plus a mohair-covered sofa bulging with plump, tasseled pillows. In one corner stood a round marble-topped table upon which were arranged a variety of knickknacks plus a large vase sprouting dried flowers and ferns. There was a small piano and a bookcase filled with leather-bound volumes. Upon a little writing desk sat an elegant three-pronged candlestick. Silver too, I supposed. The wooden furniture was elaborately carved with scrolls and brackets. Everything—walls, floor, and furniture—was dark red, brown, or tan. The room's feel was bloated wealth.

Seated in the middle of it all was Mrs. Von Macht. She did not appear as solemn as when I'd first seen her. Rather, I noticed a certain energy that made me think she was excited by what we were doing.

Behind her stood a portly, sharp-eyed man, with pointed beard, and a severe—I might even say angry—face. He was dressed in black with a high, stiff, white collar and dark cravat. A variety of gold chains and seals draped over his bulging waistcoat. He struck me as a commanding being, not someone with whom I should like to tangle. He fairly glowered at us as we entered the room.

"Ah, Mr. Middleditch," said the woman. "So pleased you've come. May I introduce you to my husband, Mr. Von Macht?"

Mr. Von Macht gave a curt nod and, with no softening in his bearing, allowed nothing by way of welcome to escape his pursed lips. His introduction was followed by a moment of tense silence.

"Mr. Middleditch, sir," the man finally said, "please be advised that I don't approve of what my wife is doing. I am merely permitting her this one self-indulgence. You will do what's necessary and then remove yourself."

He might well have added, "Or I will remove you." I, for one, didn't doubt he could.

I glanced at Mrs. Von Macht. Though the smile on her face remained fixed, her eyes hinted at what I thought was fear.

"Well, then," offered Mr. Middleditch, cheerful as ever. "I suppose we should proceed?"

"You will excuse me, sir," Mr. Von Macht said. "I have business to attend."

As the man moved to go, Mrs. Von Macht bestowed a look of unmistakable anger upon her husband's back. "You'll not," she said, "forget the dinner party tonight, Frederick. The Belmonts."

"Of course not," the man replied without looking at her, and promptly left the room. No one spoke or moved until the front door shut, sufficiently loudly to suggest he wished to give notice of his departure.

Mrs. Von Macht—her face composed with effort—said, "Mr. Middleditch, I fear my husband considers my project frivolous. The pain of our daughter's loss is too much for him."

"Ah!"

"He therefore dismisses my desire as that of an emotional, superstitious woman." She gazed down at her hands, as if to gather strength. When she looked up, the smile on her lips was forced. "Now then, Mr. Middleditch," she said, "please instruct me as to what needs to be done."

Mr. Middleditch turned to me. "Horace, prepare the plates. I will set up the camera."

Mrs. Von Macht looked to the servant girl, who had remained in the background. "Pegg, show Mr. Middleditch's boy to the scullery."

"Yes, madam."

I followed the girl out of the room. As I went, I heard Mr. Middleditch say, "Now, Mrs. Von Macht, we wish your daughter to see how beautiful you are."

ELEVEN

"WOULD YOU LIKE ME to take your coat, sir?" Pegg said to me as we went along.

Though feeling a touch of panic, I managed to say, "No, thank you. I'm feeling chilly."

She darted a questioning look but continued on without saying anything. Halfway down the steps she suddenly stopped, turned, and with one hand on the banister, as if to steady herself, looked right at me.

"Please, sir," she said softly, "I wish to apologize for what I said yesterday."

"Don't worry," I said, wanting her to tell me more. "I won't repeat what you said. And please don't call me sir."

"Thank you," she murmured, and turned away.

"But Pegg," I said, "what made you say what you did?

What makes you trust me?"

She hesitated, and without looking at me said, "I am black, but I never need a mirror to know it. I see it in other people's eyes. I had only to see how you looked at me to know you respected me."

"Of course I do."

"I don't see many who do," she murmured, and continued down.

At the foot of the steps, she waited for me. "May I call you Horace?" she said, her deep, intense eyes on me.

"I would like that."

I expected her to move on. Instead, she remained where she was, quite silent. But then, as if coming to a decision, she whispered, "Horace, you need to understand. If Mrs. Von Macht heard one word of what I said, I'd be given notice."

"Why?"

"I told you, Master and Mistress will brook no resistance."

"To what?"

"To their cruel ways."

"I see," I said, though in fact I did not.

"Didn't you observe how hard Mr. Von Macht is?" Pegg went on. "He insists the house be run with perfection. Mrs. Von Macht is the same. There's no end to the faults they can find. They don't keep servants long. You mustn't think it's a house I'd choose to live in."

"But you are here," I felt obliged to say.

"I've nowhere else to go," she said, her voice shaking.

"Oh?"

"I'm an orphan," she said.

"I'm sorry to hear that."

"Master and Mistress keep me here only because if I were to be sent off, they're fearful of what I might say."

"What would you say?"

"The things I know."

"Which are?"

I waited for her to say more and she seemed on the edge of doing so. Instead, she abruptly turned and approached the door of the scullery.

I considered Pegg. Here she was, a poor girl, a servant, an orphan, yet she spoke as if she had been educated. While her rapid changes of mood were explained by her fear of the Von Machts, her mixture of fierceness, reluctance, and great emotion kept me off balance. I certainly did not think her, as Mr. Middleditch crudely put it, touched. Nor did I feel threatened by her in any way. But I will admit I had never met such a girl.

"Did you bring the key?" she asked.

I took it from my pocket and gave it to her. She unlocked the door, and after we stepped inside she closed it again firmly, then returned the key to me.

"Pegg," I said, trying to sound chatty, "what did you mean by saying the girl was not Mrs. Von Macht's daughter?"

Pegg, saying nothing, started to move away. This time,

however, I reached out and turned her back about, not harshly, you understand, but with frustration. "I really need to know," I said.

To my surprise, her eyes were full of tears.

"Pegg," I said as kindly as I could, "I promise not to repeat what you say. I just want to understand."

A struggle seemed to be going on within her. In a small voice and with a far-off look she said, "Miss Eleanora was the daughter of Mrs. Von Macht's sister. When Eleanora's mother died of cholera, Mrs. Von Macht took Eleanora in. I came with her—as a servant. Mrs. Von Macht does not pay me."

"Slavery is gone," I said.

"I'm thirteen," she replied. "And I wish to live."

"Then Eleanora was an adopted daughter," I pressed. "An orphan like you."

Pegg suddenly shook her head. "I don't wish to say more."

Frustrated, I looked about. The room appeared just as we had left it, suffused with soft yellow light. The dozen plates covered with paper—plus the round one—were lined up on the marble table, ready for the silver nitrate solution. A quick glance at the paper tabs, which would show me that there had been a disturbance, informed me that all was as I had left it.

I looked around. Pegg was watching me. Deciding to risk another question, I said, "You said Eleanora died because the Von Machts neglected her greatly. That they wouldn't get her a doctor. Just tell me about that."

When Pegg only pressed her lips together, I decided it would be best to leave the subject. In any case, I felt pressure to get on with my work. I turned to the plates.

From our apparatus box I took out a two-inch-deep porcelain tray. I poured the silver nitrate bath into it and then quickly covered the tray with a solid lid. That done, I took out the wooden sleeves for the plates.

Under Pegg's watchful eyes I pulled back the paper from the first plate, and gasped. A jagged line with a gap of perhaps a quarter of an inch split the glass into two pieces.

"It's broken!" I cried, and turned upon the girl. "Did you come in here? Did you do this?"

The force of my accusation made her step back and lift a hand, as if avoiding a blow. "I didn't! I swear I didn't. You have the only key."

"There must be more than one."

"I don't know of another. There's just me, Cook, Mrs. Quinn, and Morgan the carriage man. None of us are permitted to have keys. Master doesn't allow it," said Pegg. "No one dares disobey him. I'm sure no one came into the room. You just said all was in order."

In haste I examined the other plates—including my round one. They were all fine.

"It must have been me," I allowed. And indeed, plates were fragile. "I'm sorry," I said. "I shouldn't have accused you. It's only that this never happened before. Anyway, we have enough plates. Please go to Mr. Middleditch and ask him if he's ready."

"Thank you," said Pegg, glad, I thought, to escape.

Just as she reached the door, I looked up and said, "Pegg, how can you be so sure the girl died of neglect?"

"When she died," she replied, "I was with her."

"Who else was there?"

"No one," she said, and fled.

Not knowing what to make of that answer, I made myself concentrate on the plates.

First, I prepared the hyposulfite of soda fixing solution, which would set the images. Next, I put out sheets of blotting paper. Third, I lay the round glass in the porcelain tray and gently moved it about for some three minutes. It took that long for the silver nitrate bits to stick to the collodion.

That accomplished, I put the round plate on the blotting paper. The yellow light kept it from darkening. I followed the same steps with each of the other plates.

By the time the last plate was readied, the round plate was damp as needed. Working quickly, I pulled out my spy camera, unscrewed the back, set the plate in, and closed it up. That, at least, was ready. Whether I was ready was quite another matter. I had been worried before I came. The girl—the troubling things she said—had only increased my tension. I desired nothing more than to be out of the house.

But there were photographs to be taken. And for the first time in my life I would take them.

TWELVE

I PUT THE OTHER DAMP PLATES into their wooden sleeves, stacked them, and carried the lot upstairs. As I went, I looked about anew but still saw no other pictures of the girl. So far it seemed Pegg had spoken true.

I knocked on the parlor door and received permission to enter. The room was somewhat altered. One of the chairs now stood before the black iron fireplace. Mrs. Von Macht was sitting in it, the look on her face holding something of a smile, if a controlled one. I could not decipher it.

Mr. Middleditch had placed her in such a position that there would be an array of dried flowers behind and to one side of her. I had no doubt a ghostly image would fit in the empty space right at the woman's shoulder. The three-pronged candlestick was also there.

The large wooden camera box was on its tripod, its lens

extended. At the rear of the camera, under the black cloth, Mr. Middleditch was framing and focusing Mrs. Von Macht by pushing and pulling the lens billows back and forth.

Mr. Middleditch peeked out from under the cloth. "Ah, the plates." He took them from me. "Now, Horace," he said with a wink that only I could see, "be so good as to get the cleaning cloth." There was no such thing as a "cleaning cloth." I was being told to leave the room and take the secret pictures.

Hoping I was not blushing with the lie, I muttered, "Yes, sir," and stepped from the room into the hall. Each of Mr. Middleditch's exposures—the time it took to catch the image on the plate—would take at least three minutes. He had eleven plates. In other words, I had thirty or so minutes to do my task.

After making sure I was not being observed (I was most anxious about Pegg), I pushed the camera's lens tube through a buttonhole of my coat. But since the painting was set about six feet above the floor, I had to angle the lens up. That required putting my hands into my coat so as to aim the camera. I did so, took a deep breath, and pushed the shutter lever. There was a tiny click.

I had taken my very first picture.

I can't deny that in spite of my nervousness I was thrilled. Had I not—finally—become a photographer?

I decided to take another photo because I was not absolutely sure I had aimed the camera correctly. Besides, nobody was there to see what I was doing. And I really was excited by what I was doing.

The shutter tripped a second time.

With two pictures taken, the question was, Where next? Frankly, I still didn't know whether to believe Pegg, and I wanted to accept what Mrs. Von Macht had said: "I have many painted images of her about my house." Yet I had seen none in the room which Mrs. Von Macht and Mr. Middleditch now occupied, nor any on the lower floor. Going into the adjacent dining room would be much too perilous. That left the upper floors.

Heart pounding, I stood at the bottom of the steps. After checking anew to make sure I was unobserved, I started up. Happily the thick carpeting muffled my steps.

Along the stairwell walls there were other pictures, but none of the girl.

The steps led me to a U-turn by way of a little landing. There was a small table upon which sat a vase holding flowers. Prints of Roman ruins adorned the wall.

No images of Eleanora.

I reached the second floor. I saw some gas light sconces on the wall, but with nothing lit it was quite dim. Such light as there was came from behind, through a large window that looked over the rear alleyway. Before me I could see three rooms: one at the front of the house and two leading off from a hallway. All had closed doors.

More pictures on the wall: images of flowers, of landscapes, silhouettes of George Washington and General Tyler. None of Eleanora Von Macht.

Mystified, perhaps wanting to prove Pegg wrong, I was more determined than ever to complete my search. I went to the first door and put my hand to the doorknob. Hardly wishing to come upon Mr. Von Macht, I leaned against the door and listened. Hearing nothing, I put pressure on the doorknob. It turned easily. With the greatest caution, I pushed the door open a crack and listened again. Still nothing. Edging the door open farther and holding my breath, I peeked in.

The room was deserted. I saw a large oak desk and chair. Bookcases filled with business ledgers. Unlit lamps. My guess: Mr. Von Macht's private study.

With many pictures on the walls.

I stepped inside and cast a quick glance about at the pictures: framed certificates, heraldry, and naval pictures—warships and the like. Of Eleanora, the daughter his wife said he grieved so deeply, not one.

Baffled, I went on to the next room. As before, I approached with care. It proved to be a bedroom, furnished lavishly with a large four-post bed, dressing table, chairs, armoire, and chandelier. The appointments of comfort and wealth. They did love candlelight! On the wall, framed pictures. Of flowers. Of birds. None of Eleanora.

The third room was a bathroom. I did not expect to see any images there, and indeed there were none.

I retreated to the hallway. It was bad enough being where I should not be. Worse, I was as yet unable to do the job I'd been asked to do.

Another flight of steps led to a third floor. Though these steps were neither as wide nor as grand as the first-floor steps, I felt compelled to investigate. I went up. The third-floor ceiling was low, with plain bare walls. Along a narrow hallway were four rooms, doors closed. I checked them one by one. The first two rooms were small and drably furnished: narrow bed, table, chair, and chest. No room for any more. I took them to be servants' rooms.

The third room was the smallest. No furniture. Old, dry, wooden floor, walls, and ceiling. A storeroom, perhaps, but nothing stored. Indeed, quite desolate.

The next, final room contained an undersized and narrow bed, a chair, and a table. On that table was a propped-up picture. Though small, I instantly recognized it as a faded photograph of Eleanora Von Macht.

At last!

The face—showing the girl at an earlier age than the portrait below—revealed joy. That is, Eleanora was wearing a large sunbonnet, a light-colored dress. A smile was on her face. Moreover, the image was at table height, making it easy to focus upon with my hidden camera. Moving quickly, I photographed it.

I was still gazing at the face when I heard a sound behind me. Taken by surprise, I spun about to see who was there. As I did, I tripped the shutter a fourth time.

Pegg had come into the room.

THIRTEEN

WE STARED AT EACH OTHER: I with much embarrassment, she openmouthed with surprise.

Pegg spoke first and she did so with anger.

"What are you doing here?"

Mr. Middleditch's words came to mind. "I . . . I was just admiring the house," I managed to say.

She glared at me. "There's nothing to admire here."

At a loss, I turned and pointed to the picture. "There's that."

The anger seemed to drain from Pegg. Tears welled in her eyes. "She was my darling sister," she said softly. "She had the room next door."

"She . . . was up *here?*" I said. "In that . . . empty room?"

"Those were her happy times," said Pegg. "When we

were alone together."

I was bewildered. Could this girl be "touched" after all, as Mr. Middleditch had suggested? I found it impossible to believe that Eleanora Von Macht, daughter of such wealth, would have lived in so mean a place. Nor that this black servant girl would be her sister. "And was that," I asked, trying to draw her out, "when she told you she had died of neglect?"

"Of course not," she returned, her voice instantly tinged with fierceness. "She told me that after she died."

I stared at her. "How was she able to do that?"

"She whispered it into my heart."

"Stood there and *told* you?"

"She was dead," returned Pegg. "I know that. But since I knew her better than anyone, I can always hear her voice." Then, wistfully, she added, "I would give anything to speak to her again."

I almost said—but didn't—my father's refrain: "Let the dead bury the dead."

She sensed something of my thoughts. "You don't believe me, do you?" she said.

I saw no point in arguing. For as my father also used to say: "Don't debate the superstitious. Pity them." And I needed to get back to Mr. Middleditch.

"I'm wanted below," I said, and I fear I went rudely past the girl as I made my way to the first floor.

My timing was good. Mr. Middleditch had just concluded his photo session. The exposed plates were stacked. Mrs. Von Macht was sitting in much the same way as before.

"Ah! There you are, Horace," said Mr. Middleditch, his face working hard to suppress a smile when I appeared. It was a relief he did not wink at me. He nodded to the plates. "They're ready for you."

So I was not able to tell him that I had only taken three pictures. I simply gathered up the boxed plates and went down to the scullery.

Once inside the room I locked the door. Not only did I not want Pegg to come in and distract me with her strangeness, I truly needed to concentrate. Besides, I needed to take off my coat and remove the secret camera from around my neck.

I began my work by pouring the developing solution into one porcelain tray, the fixing solution into another. Next I ran some water into one of the sinks. Then I took the exposed plates from their shields and put them into the developer fluid—pyrogallic acid and silver iodide.

There is something almost magical about the developing of a photographic image. Consider: You stand quietly in a room with a dim yellow light that fills the air with an enchanting twilight glow. That glow always seems to transport me to another place, a demiworld where images, like shy spirits, lie in wait.

Holding your breath, you peer into a chemical brew. Not so very different, I suppose, from sorcerers of old when they gazed into their magical potions. Gently you slide the exposed but blank glass plate into this chemical bath. You wait for something to appear as if waiting on the shore of a mist-shrouded lake.

Slowly, a shadowy image begins to reveal itself. It's as if the shadow were coming from some mystic depth, emerging from another world, little by little, taking bodily shape and form until that shadow becomes . . . real. Just what one would expect—would want—from a ghost.

But the image on the glass is backward—that's to say, what is dark is light, what is light is dark—a negative image, which only enhances its otherworldliness.

During the whole process, you must watch the image intently. Too much developer and the negative turns as black as soot, becoming irretrievably lost. It's as if the image, coming as it does from an unreachable void, plunges back into the emptiness from whence it came. Unless you hold the shadow and embrace it tightly, it will vanish—forever.

So it was then: As each image came into view, I had to determine its peak, after which I snatched it from the developer and plunged the plate into the fixing solution. By so doing, I locked each image in time—caught it in visible life.

Though it all appears magical, even mystical, the true wonder is that the process is entirely chemical. Human reason—my reason—controlled it. What a sense of mastery it gave me! I, Horace Carpetine, could turn a shadow into something real.

Once the developing process had been accomplished, the plates went into a water bath to wash away any remaining silver nitrate, and thus make certain no further development took place.

One by one I did this for Mr. Middleditch's eleven plates. All his negative images appeared good. He would be pleased.

After I'd finished processing Mr. Middleditch's images, I turned to the circular plate, the secret pictures I'd made. In this case all three of my images would be on one plate.

My first pictures! Never mind the circumstances. I was excited.

With great care—consider how much depended on what I had accomplished!—I placed the round plate into the developing bath, then watched and waited with great expectation. Almost simultaneously the images of a girl's face rose up before my eyes: one, two, and three . . . four.

Four!

There is an ancient, and surely worn-out expression, that of not believing one's own eyes. Such was my state as I stared at the small, round glass plate and its four images. What I was seeing made no sense.

I struggled to find an explanation.

In fact, I stared at the images for so long I had to plunge

the disk into the fixing solution before I lost them utterly. As they lay in the water bath, I made myself recall the pictures I had taken.

I had begun by taking two pictures in the hallway—of the portrait. The third was taken in Pegg's room—the small picture that she had on the table.

I was certain I had only taken those three images. Nonetheless there were—I could see quite plainly—four images.

How could that be?

Then—with great relief—I remembered: When Pegg came into the room, I had been so startled I swung about in haste and tripped the shutter. In so doing I must have taken a picture of Pegg. That would be the fourth image.

My emotions calmed. I had found a rational explanation for what occurred.

I gazed into the water. Because the pictures on the round plate were quite small, negative, and in water—the identity of that fourth image remained unclear. Surely, since no one else was in that room, it had to be Pegg.

But was it?

FOURTEEN

BEFORE LEAVING MRS. VON MACHT, Mr. Middleditch made an appointment for the following Thursday to bring his finished photograph.

As the carriage pulled away, I said, "Mr. Middleditch—"

He silenced me with a gesture reminding me that the driver might hear. But as soon as we reached our rooms, he said, "Did you get them?" Meaning images of the girl's portraits.

"I did, but—"

"Did they process well?"

"Yes, sir, but—"

"But what?"

"When Mrs. Von Macht said there were portraits of the girl all over the house, she misspoke. There was only that one in the hallway."

"Not possible," he said.

"It's true," I insisted, and told him where I had gone.

"Other than the hallway—not one other picture?"

"Well, one."

"Ha! I knew you were mistaken!"

"It was in the servant girl's room. The very top floor."

"Didn't I tell you that girl was jealous of the dear departed? Were you able to photograph it?"

"Yes, sir."

"Then how many pictures did you take—in all?"

I hesitated. "Three."

He fussed with his mustache. "Let's hope that will be enough," he said. "Now go and varnish the negatives."

Varnishing the negative images was done for protection, so they would remain free from dust and scratches. Compared to the other chemicals, I found the smell of varnish sweet.

As I did the round plate, I held it up to the light, trying to gain some sense of that fourth image. But the images were so small and negative, I still could not determine whose picture I had taken. And until the varnish hardened—twenty-four hours—I could not use the negative to make the larger positive prints that would allow me to see them distinctly. I left them to dry.

Next morning, Sunday, I went to my weekly dinner with

my family. I used the opportunity to take my father aside and told him what was happening, at least some of it.

"Father," I said, "if an employer is taking advantage of a customer, how should his employee react?"

"A most interesting question. First I should ask, is the employer doing something illegal?"

"I . . . I don't think so."

"Second: Will it harm anyone?"

"It might upset someone."

"'Upset' is an emotional response. You and I are rationalists, Horace. We observe things clearly, scientifically. We do not get upset. So, now, will it truly harm anyone?"

"I suppose not."

"Will the employer's actions do harm to the employee?"

"I . . . don't think so."

"Then I conclude this: Do nothing. It might jeopardize your employment. But—learn that not all men are honest. Just as important, tell yourself that you will see things rationally and scientifically and that you will act honestly and uphold the highest code of personal behavior." He wagged a finger at me. "Failure brings excuses to the weak but strength to the strong."

It was after six o'clock when I returned to the Charlton Street rooms. By then it was dark. I let myself in with my key, lit a candle, and saw that Mr. Middleditch had not returned. Nor was there any note as to when he would get back. Nothing unusual there.

Normally I would have gone to bed, most likely reading some of *The Silver Sunbeam*, for I was always keen to learn more about photography. That night, however, I was too consumed by curiosity about my first photographs.

Happily the varnish-coated plates were hard. And once I committed myself to make positive images, I began the process in earnest. My desire was to accomplish everything before Mr. Middleditch returned.

In the room we used for such work, I set up the porcelain basins beneath the regular dim yellow lantern light. Then I processed Mr. Middleditch's work—the eleven images he had taken of Mrs. Von Macht. They came out quite well. He had done a creditable job.

I did see that each image contained the candlestick. That struck me as odd. I made a mental note to ask Mr. Middleditch about it.

Next I placed my round glass negative plate above a treated card, exposed it to bright, focused yellow lamplight, and then slipped the card into the developing solution.

As always, the images blossomed up before my eyes in wonderful fashion. I then set the paper in the fixing solution and washed the whole print with care. Finally, I set the circular print on blotting paper and brought normal light back into the room. Only then was I able to closely examine the images I'd taken with the secret camera.

I had produced four small images set around in semicircular fashion—rather like a half moon. Not surprisingly, the first image was very much out of focus. Blurry. Then, progressively, I did better. This is not to say the last was a sharp image—far from it—but there was considerably less haziness from first to last.

One by one I examined the pictures:

The first two images were the Eleanora Von Macht of the portrait that hung in the hallway. Aside from not being in focus, they were rather distorted—but I had angled the camera up. I was not sure they would work for Mr. Middleditch's need.

The third image I'd taken was of the photograph in Pegg's room—the one that sat upon her table—the cheerful face of Eleanora Von Macht beneath the large sunbonnet. Insofar as it had perched chest-high, it was more in focus than my earlier efforts. That it was somewhat fuzzy added a ghostlike quality. I thought Mr. Middleditch might be able to use it.

Finally I examined that fourth image. Or rather, I should say I stared at it. By my rational understanding, if the image of anyone had been captured in that accidental picture, it should have been Pegg's.

Gazing up at me was the face of Eleanora Von Macht.

I was so startled I nearly dropped the card. I blinked and shook my head—as if to break loose from the impossibility. But when I looked again, the image of Eleanora

Von Macht's face remained.

I gazed at it for a long time. There was no question as to whose face it was. But this fourth image was altogether different from the third.

Item: In Pegg's image Eleanora wore a bonnet. The girl in the fourth picture had no bonnet.

Item: Pegg's image had a smile. The girl in the fourth picture was angry, frowning.

Item: Pegg's image revealed a light-colored dress. In the fourth image the girl wore what appeared to be a dark, perhaps black, frock.

In short, a different image altogether!

My eyes shifted from one to the other with growing agitation. Gradually I realized that the fourth image was also in sharper focus. Far from what it should have been perhaps, but certainly better. This was odd, because my taking it was an accident.

Which was all to say that in some fashion, in some way, I had photographed an entirely new image of Eleanora Von Macht, one that didn't appear on the hallway painting or on Pegg's table.

But that was impossible. Eleanora was dead.

FIFTEEN

Next morning I woke tired and uneasy. Right away I recalled the fourth image and knew I did not wish to tell Mr. Middleditch about it. Aside from my own puzzlement, it touched on Pegg, and I did not want to give him an opportunity for more of his insulting remarks. But right after breakfast he asked me if I was ready to print the images he had taken.

"They are already printed," I said.

"Horace, you are a wonder! Sometimes I think I should let you do everything. Let's have a look."

First I brought out the pictures he took, the formal portraits of Mrs. Von Macht. He examined each of the eleven carefully.

"These two are particularly flattering of the lady," he said, setting them aside. "I think she'll care for them a great deal.

And do you see, Horace, how I left space for . . ." That infernal wink. "You know what."

"Sir, why is the candlestick in all the pictures?"

"Mrs. Von Macht requested it: she said it was the last gift from the departed girl. Well, then," he went on, "so far, so good. Now, bring in the pictures you took." There was something sly in his voice—like a little boy smirking over an impending practical joke.

I had no choice. I brought in the round image, took a deep breath, and handed it to him.

He studied the sheet intently. "I thought you said you only took three pictures."

"I was mistaken," I said, trying to be as neutral as possible.

"They are not in good focus, Horace."

"My first pictures, sir. And it was hard to sight the spy camera."

"Fair enough. We might say they already are ghostlike. Now, these first two," he said, "they are the portrait in the hallway—am I right?"

"Yes, sir."

"Perhaps too obviously so. This one?"

"I took it in the servant girl's room."

"Ah! So you said."

"And this one . . . ?" He pointed to the fourth image.

I could not even look at him. "I'm not sure."

"What do you mean, you're not sure?"

I didn't think he would be very helpful—or sympathetic—but I wanted to be honest. I said, "I must have taken it, but . . . I didn't aim it at any picture."

"Horace! Don't be a blockhead! There must have been. The girl's face is here. And it's a different image."

I gazed at him. "Sir, I didn't see her."

He shrugged. "Well, it doesn't matter. I don't care for that fourth face anyway. Mean-spirited. Almost angry, don't you think? No, it won't do. I'm sure Mrs. Von Macht would prefer a cheerful ghost."

How like the man to be so uninterested in the puzzle of the fourth photo!

"Now, this one," he went on, indicating my image of the picture on Pegg's table, "*will* work. In any case Eleanora is jolly though somewhat blurred. Perhaps a useful combination. Not grave." He grinned. "Horace, that was a pun! Don't be so gloomy! Now come, we really have work to do."

By work, he meant creating his "spirit image."

It took considerable time.

First he made new images of Mrs. Von Macht. Next, he overlaid my small image of Eleanora on the same paper. In other words, from two negatives, he made one positive. The result: there was Mrs. Von Macht, and hovering over her left shoulder was . . . Eleanora. She looked, I must admit, very ghostlike.

"It needs to be perfect," he proclaimed, and set to work as hard as I ever had seen him labor, producing a fair number of composite images until he was satisfied. He was like a little boy, so intent upon a complex practical joke he gave no thought as to the possible consequences. The joke was all!

In this manner he worked all of one day and much of the next until he achieved the desired effect.

What had he achieved? Mr. Middleditch had posed Mrs. Von Macht in her parlor. Sitting, she looked very fine in her fashionable dark gown, a composed, handsome, wealthy woman, tinted by a touch of sadness. All credit to Mr. Middleditch for capturing a quality that I had no doubt would be very pleasing, indeed flattering, to the woman.

But Mr. Middleditch had done a very clever thing, utter fraud though it was. He had arranged the vase and candlestick on the table behind the woman, and then superimposed the vague, smiling face of Eleanora among them.

When you glanced at the whole picture, you did not see the girl right away. Your eyes first took in Mrs. Von Macht. Only gradually did you discover the ghost image—sufficiently indistinct that one could deny seeing anything at all. Yet she was there.

Mr. Middleditch was, as he had promised, about to spring a very clever trick.

"I can't wait to bring this to Mrs. Von Macht," he announced with glee.

"When will that be?" I asked.

"Tomorrow. And Horace, unless I am very wrong, at some point she'll ask me if I see something."

"What will you say?"

"Why, nothing, of course. This must be her discovery. I suppose," he mused, "she might even ask what you see."

"Me?"

"You must be as silent as the *grave*," he said with a laugh. And when he did, I made up my mind. If the woman did ask me what I saw, I would say there was something there.

That created a predicament for me. I was determined to tell the truth—but what was the truth? That the image was a trick? Surely Mr. Middleditch's photograph was. But where had that fourth image of Eleanora come from?

Sitting on my bed, quite alone, I stared at the face of Eleanora I had photographed—the fourth image—trying to find a reasonable explanation for its being there.

I could not.

SIXTEEN

THE NEXT DAY at the appointed time, Mr. Middleditch went to Mrs. Von Macht's home. I went with him. I'm not exactly sure why he wanted me. I suspect it was vanity. I suspect Mr. Middleditch wished me at his side to observe the swindle take effect. How like the man to want my admiration!

I was more than willing to go, wishing to see how the woman would react. I also wanted to speak to Pegg so as to learn more about what she'd said regarding Eleanora. Were Pegg's statements—other than there being no pictures of Eleanora in the house—true? In all of this I was hoping to make some sense of that amazing fourth picture. The point being, I was now convinced something very odd was going on in the Von Macht household and, let me confess it, I really wished to know what it was.

We arrived at the house with Mr. Middleditch carrying his photos in a black portfolio tied neatly with a red ribbon. He pulled the bell. Pegg opened the door. She did her little curtsy, saying, "Madam is expecting you."

But unlike our previous visit, when Pegg only glanced at Mr. Middleditch, this time she looked directly at me. Her glance unnerved me. It seemed to proclaim that she and I shared something, some knowledge private just to us. Yet, what that understanding was, remained a mystery to me.

Pegg led us into the front parlor, where Mrs. Von Macht was waiting. I followed a few steps behind Mr. Middleditch. Pegg remained in the room, taking a place in a corner out of sight. It was quite warm.

Mrs. Von Macht was dressed in a gown a little more glamorous than she had worn previously. Her face was not nearly so pale either—less powder, perhaps—displaying healthy, pink cheeks. Whereas the scent of perfume was a little stronger, the mourning armband was gone. Upon her lap lay embroidery work. But I noticed that while she held a needle in hand, as if caught in the middle of work, the needle bore no thread.

Her husband was not present, for which I, for one, was grateful. There was too much anger in the man.

As we came forward, I glanced to Mrs. Von Macht's left, at the table where the vase with dried flowers and the candlestick remained. There, among these things, I saw a face—Eleanora Von Macht's face.

Shocked is barely the word for what I experienced. Such was my great fright that I will swear my heart momentarily stopped beating. In that space of time I could neither breathe nor swallow. The hair at the back of my neck prickled. Not willing to believe what I was seeing, I closed my eyes, but could not resist looking again. The face was gone.

Struggling to control my emotions and my trembling body, my first thought was that my eyes had simply deceived me. I turned toward Mrs. Von Macht. Nothing in her demeanor suggested she had seen anything. I looked to Mr. Middleditch. No reaction there either. I glanced at Pegg. The same.

I told myself that my mind was merely playing tricks and quickly found a rational answer: Over the past few days, I had been continually seeing the ghostly image of Eleanora that Mr. Middleditch had concocted in that very same spot. What I was seeing, I told myself, was simply what was on my mind—not something actually there.

These thoughts took only seconds. In fact, it takes longer to describe the ghastly moment than to live it. In any case, I was brought back to my senses—senses now sparked, as a lit fuse—by hearing Mr. Middleditch say, "Mrs. Von Macht, how do you do?" He made his little bow.

"Very well, Mr. Middleditch," she returned in a perfectly civil tone, while holding out her delicate white hand for him to touch. "I hope I find you well."

"Very well, madam. I thank you." After briefly holding the

woman's fingertips, he straightened. "Madam, I think you will be very pleased with the results of our photo session." I could almost see his bulldog's tail wag.

"I expect to be."

The thought struck me—considering her unthreaded needle and his posturing—that they were both playing games, though neither knew that about the other. But while I knew his game very well, what, I wondered, was hers?

"May I rest the portfolio there?" Mr. Middleditch said, indicating the sofa.

"Please do."

A true showman, Mr. Middleditch made a little bow, and then, with an elaborate movement just slow enough to create anticipation, he set the portfolio on the couch. With unnecessary fuss he untied the ribbons, spread the portfolio leaves, picked up the single photograph he'd brought, and with the greatest delicacy carried it across the room. Another little bow. Then, holding the image with two hands, he offered the picture to the woman. Moreover, he deliberately presented the image blank side up, so she would have to turn it over and take it in whole.

Mr. P. T. Barnum, the circus man, had nothing on Mr. Middleditch!

Mrs. Von Macht took the picture, turned the photo over, and, with her head tilted slightly forward, gazed upon the image that Mr. Middleditch had created.

The room grew very still.

SEVENTEEN

I DON'T KNOW HOW LONG Mrs. Von Macht stared at the picture. Only after some time had passed did I hear a sharp intake of breath. Even so, she did not move for a long while but continued to gaze down, as if transfixed.

"Is it to your . . . liking?" Mr. Middleditch asked.

When Mrs. Von Macht finally lifted her head, her eyes were open wider than normal. Her cheeks were flushed, too, while her lips were parted, as if she were in need of air.

I had no doubt: She had discovered her daughter's ghost-like image. And what I saw on the woman's face was fright.

She composed herself with visible effort. "Mr. Middleditch—," she said, only to stop.

She stood up abruptly and, still holding the photograph in her hands, moved toward the front windows and drew aside one of the heavy drapes, thereby allowing some natural light to fall upon the image. She resumed her intense scrutiny of it in silence. I am sure I heard her breathing quicken.

"Is there," asked Mr. Middleditch, "something . . . wrong?"

I knew him well enough to perceive that he was now a little concerned—as if only then did he realize the peril in which he had placed himself.

"It . . . it is a lovely picture," Mrs. Von Macht said, but the words came out in a ragged whisper as if she were not fully in command of her voice.

"Thank you," said Mr. Middleditch, making his little bow. "When the subject is so . . . attractive, the photograph must follow."

"You are . . . kind." The woman's voice was small, unusually uncertain.

With a sudden gesture she held out the photograph. "Mr. Middleditch," she asked, "have you examined this?"

"Examined it?" he said, hesitating before taking the picture into his large hands. "I'm not sure I understand. I made it."

"Mr. Middleditch—in the photograph—look behind me. Among the flowers. Do you . . . see . . . anything . . . odd?"

I stared at him, my whole body tense, wondering what he would do.

Mr. Middleditch made a show of bending over the picture, muttering, "I see . . . flowers. The candlestick." He looked up, all innocence. "Is there . . . something else?"

Mrs. Von Macht frowned. She had been pale before. Now she looked flushed. "Show it to your boy!" she snapped.

"But—"

"Show it!"

He winced under the lash of her command, but complied. And though he did give it to me, he avoided looking at me directly.

My heart pounding, I took the image and gazed at it, my eyes immediately focusing on the vague face of Eleanora. I was quite prepared, contrary to Mr. Middleditch's instructions, to say I did see something. But when I looked, what I saw was *not* the picture *I* had taken, *not* the picture Mr. Middleditch had inserted, but a completely different face!

I stared at it, utterly amazed. Beyond question, it was Eleanora Von Macht. But it was a very angry face, the same face I had momentarily seen among the flowers when I entered the room. Was this another trick of my mind? All I could do was gaze at it, stupefied, quite unable to speak.

As if from a different world, I heard the woman's voice. "Do you see something, boy?"

I could only shake my head.

Mrs. Von Macht reached out for the picture.

With a trembling hand, I let her have the picture, watching as she gazed down at it anew. What, I wondered, was *she* seeing?

The silence in the room created a terrible tension.

"Madam," said Mr. Middleditch, "are you . . . dissatisfied with the picture? Does it lack something?"

Mrs. Von Macht looked up. There was no question that there was fright in her eyes. Indeed, for a few moments she did not reply, as if she were unable to speak. "You may . . . you may send my husband . . . a bill," she finally stammered.

It was a dismissal.

Mr. Middleditch was surprised. "Are you quite sure—"

"Mr. Middleditch!" said the woman. "You may go."

There was no choice. We had to leave. Pegg emerged from her corner and opened the door for us.

As we stepped out of the parlor, the door shutting firmly behind us, I struggled to know what to think. What was it I had seen? Had Mrs. Von Macht seen the "spirit image" or not? I would have sworn she had, but did she believe she was being duped or did she believe she was seeing a ghost?

Pegg led us toward the front door. Neither I nor Mr. Middleditch spoke. I tried to catch Pegg's eyes, but she would not look my way.

Just as we reached the front door, a voice called from behind. "Mr. Middleditch!"

We turned. It was Mrs. Von Macht. She was in the hall-way.

"Come back here!"

Mr. Middleditch hesitated—as if uncertain whether to

return or flee. When I saw him make a slight shift toward the door as if to escape, I decided. Wanting answers, I turned back. Mr. Middleditch had little choice but to follow.

Pegg hastened to lead the way.

We returned to the parlor. Mrs. Von Macht was standing by the window, back to us, staring out. The sun from the uncovered window glinted on her very black hair. The photograph lay upon the chair.

"I fear," ventured Mr. Middleditch, "I have not pleased you."

A slight shift of the woman's shoulders suggested she was gathering strength. Finally she turned about. She was pale, breathing with difficulty. One hand pressed against her throat. "Mr. Middleditch," she said. "I must know . . . was that the photograph you took . . . in these rooms?"

"Of course, madam. But if you are not happy with—"

"Mr. Middleditch, pick up the photograph."

"But—"

"Pick it up," she cried. "Look at it!"

He did so, and gazed down, as if studying it.

"Do you notice," she demanded, "anything else in that image?"

I could almost see him calculating the best response. "It's enough, dear lady, that I see you—"

"No flattery, Mr. Middleditch! It ill becomes you."

The man had the decency to blush.

"Then I don't under—"

"Mr. Middleditch, do you see nothing . . . unusual in that photograph?"

Again the man acted as if he were studying the picture. "Madam," he said. "I confess I don't. Is there something I should see?"

Of course he was pretending. For her part I was sure she was trying to decide if she should reveal what she saw.

"Pegg," she suddenly said, "leave the room. Take the boy with you."

Pegg's eyes met mine and I followed her out.

EIGHTEEN

THE MOMENT WE WENT into the hallway, Pegg whispered, "Quiet!" and pressed an ear to the door.

I stood there, not daring to utter a word.

I'm uncertain how long Pegg listened, but she suddenly pulled away and leaned toward me. "What made you react so when you saw the photograph?"

"Pegg," I whispered, "I think I saw Eleanora."

"Eleanora!" The expression on Pegg's face was one of astonishment.

"I'm sure of it."

"Where?"

"In there," I said, beckoning to the parlor. "Twice."

"I don't understand."

"Just part of her really, her face, first among the dried

flowers behind Mrs. Von Macht. Then in the photograph he gave her. "

For a moment she could not speak. Then she said, "Are you sure?"

"Yes! But the image in the photograph and the face in the flowers were different."

"But that's im—"

"It was your Eleanora."

She stared at me. "This evening," she suddenly said in a fierce, whispered voice. "Nine o'clock. Come to the servant's door under the stoop. I must know more. Will you come?"

"I'll try, but—"

She put a hand on my arm. "Shhh!"

The next moment the door swung out. Mr. Middleditch, his face betraying no emotion, stepped out of the room. "Horace, come along."

The interior door slammed shut behind him while Mr. Middleditch hurried toward the front door. Pegg darted forward to reach it and hold it open.

He went out. I looked to Pegg as I followed. Her mouth shaped the words: *Nine o'clock*. I nodded, went out of the house, and caught up with Mr. Middleditch on the pavement.

"Mr. Middleditch, sir—"

"No talk!"

Breaking into a brisk walk, he headed downtown so rapidly I had to hurry to keep up. All the while I kept glancing up at his face, trying to guess what had transpired when he was alone in the room with Mrs. Von Macht. At the same time I was attempting to make sense of what I had experienced.

He did not stop until we had gone a few blocks.

Then he burst into laughter.

Not polite laughter either, but explosive glee, with much hand clapping, even—for the man was really one great cliché—wiping tears of mirth away.

I stood there, baffled.

"Sir?" I ventured when his laughter had subsided into giggles. "What happened?"

"What happened?" he echoed, struggling to gain some composure. "Why, perfection itself! Oh, Horace, if I may say so, I am the Edwin Booth of photographers." He was comparing himself to the greatest actor of the age.

"What do you mean?"

"Horace, not only did Mrs. Von Macht see the image, she truly believes it's a ghostly manifestation of her daughter. What's more, Horace, it took her"—he began to laugh again—"it took her considerable time to convince me—to convince *me*, Horace—that the smiling face of her daughter was truly there! Oh, Horace, you must, you really must applaud my acting skills."

The smiling face! His words made me realize he had seen

yet a *different* face from the one I had. Then what face had Mrs. Von Macht seen?

I said, "Was Mrs. Von Macht . . . glad it was there?"

"Glad? Why, do you know, Horace, I think she was . . . alarmed. But then, I suppose any parent would be alarmed if they saw the ghostly image of a beloved dead child appearing in a photograph. I can imagine my feelings if I saw my late, unlamented father hovering over my shoulder in a photograph." He laughed.

"Sir," I said, "what will happen next?"

"I'll send her a bill. Believe me, Horace, it shall be a hefty one, too. I worked hard, didn't I?"

"Will that be the end of it, then?" I would have been greatly relieved to have it be so.

He became thoughtful. "I predict . . . Horace . . . Yes! I believe that in a few days I shall hear from Mrs. Von Macht again. Let's see: She'll ask me to call on her. I'll be happy— of course I will—to meet with her. This time, perhaps with her husband. Can you imagine, Horace, what will happen when she shows him the picture? Rather an angry fellow, wasn't he? Never mind!

"Very well, then, here's my prediction: She'll want more photographs. To make sure it was not an accident." He began to laugh again.

"Will you make them?"

"Make them? Horace, I intend to make many such spirit

pictures and thereby make my fortune! For here's another forecast. Within one month's time I shall hear from one of her friends who has lost someone or other. My goodness, children are dying all the time. I know, pitiful. But what's that saying? 'It's an ill wind that blows no good.' Exactly! All right, then. Let some profit blow my way. Come along! We really must dine again at O'Tooly's. This time I shall treat you to a plate of oysters! Horace, we shall make a night of it.

"My young friend," he cried, clapping me on the shoulder, "you did very well!"

Oh, how I detested him then! How his willingness to mock and profit by another's grief disgusted me! How his smugness put himself first in all things! And beyond all else, he was so bent upon swindle, he was utterly unaware that something extraordinary was happening.

NINETEEN

WE CONTINUED WALKING as all the while I turned over in my mind how I might proceed. More than anything I was determined to meet with Pegg that night. At length I said, "Mr. Middleditch, sir."

"What's that, Horace?"

"Perhaps you'll excuse me, sir, but I'd rather not dine out. My . . . stomach is a little too queasy for oysters."

"Have a porterhouse steak."

"I'd just as soon not eat at all, sir."

"Suit yourself, Horace," he said, still in high glee. "I would have enjoyed your company. But if you're determined not to come, be aware, I'll eat your portion."

"I hope you will, sir."

With Mr. Middleditch so full of energy, we moved on

quickly. It was only as we approached our rooms that I said, "Mr. Middleditch, sir, there is something that puzzles me."

"What's that?"

"The image in the picture, the photograph you gave Mrs. Von Macht it . . . it wasn't right."

"What are you talking about? Of course it was right."

"The picture I took—the image from the servant girl's room—the one you used to make the double exposure was not the same face on the photograph you gave Mrs. Von Macht."

He considered me blankly. "Of course it was."

"I don't think so."

It was as if I'd told him I'd sprouted wings and could fly. "Horace," he said, "that's absurd!"

"Exactly, sir—"

"Horace," he said, clapping a hand on my shoulder, "I'm afraid it's not just your stomach that's a bit off. Your head is, too. I know! You've been listening to that colored girl."

I turned away in disgust. My only hope was that Pegg could provide some explanation. But I would have to wait until nine o'clock.

Mr. Middleditch was so full of his success he could not keep still. After pacing about for a while, he bolted from our rooms with an over-the-shoulder call of "Hope you feel better!" I suspect he went off to find someone to whom he could more agreeably brag about his successful hoax.

That was fine with me. I had no desire for his company. On the contrary, I was considering quitting my apprenticeship or, I should say, him. Unfortunately, I was only too aware I would have to speak to my father about the matter, as I knew neither the terms he had established nor if he might incur a financial loss. Besides, I was fearful my father would only scoff if I tried to describe the events I had experienced.

But what really held me was this: While I could no longer deny that something extraordinary was occurring, more than anything I wanted to understand it rationally, to find some science that could explain these bizarre events. But to do so I needed to be very sure what was happening. It required patience—and Pegg.

That left me some idle hours before our meeting. Trying to use my time effectively, I repaired to our processing room and took up the circular glass negative that contained the four images I had taken with the concealed camera. From it I made a new print.

In the studio I found one of the prints Mr. Middleditch made when he constructed his spirit photograph. These were his practice prints, created before he made the one he offered to Mrs. Von Macht.

What I observed was disturbing. The circular images were, as previously noted, four in number.

Recall: The first two images were of Eleanora Von Macht's

painted portrait in the hallway of the Von Macht house.

The third image was of the picture that Pegg had in her room on her little table.

The fourth image was also of Eleanora, the one I was convinced I did not shoot but which, without doubt, was taken in Pegg's room.

Now, insofar as Mr. Middleditch had used the third image for his composite picture, I compared the print I had just made with Mr. Middleditch's practice print.

They were the same.

Therein lay a new puzzle: I was absolutely certain that when I had looked at the photo Mrs. Von Macht put into my hands, it was *not* the same image.

And what about the face I had seen—or thought I had seen—in the background when I first entered the room?

All this, in the words of Mr. Middleditch, was absurd. The only explanation based on reason was that someone or something was creating these appearances. But who? Surely not Mr. Middleditch!

Is it any wonder that I was beginning to doubt my judgment? Were not my own eyes seeing things that made no sense?

The results of my examination left me more restive than ever. Though my meeting with Pegg was still some hours away, I could no longer confine myself to our rooms. Besides, I did not want to chance an early return by Mr.

Middleditch. It would be harder to get away. So I sallied out into the city determined to pass my time as best I could. With me I took an extra print of the secret pictures. I needed to share it with Pegg. To get her response. Her reaction. I needed a reasonable explanation.

TWENTY

IT WAS ABOUT SEVEN in the evening when I set out from our rooms. The last glimmerings of twilight still held sway. The air was soothing. As I walked uptown along wide, crowded Broadway, I wanted to lose myself among the throngs. Shops were doing a brisk trade. Saloons and rum houses were overflowing. Streets were full of horse-drawn vehicles, walkways crowded with bearded or mustachioed men with top hats and bowlers. Newsboys hawked on corners. Workmen aplenty in rough cord trousers and slouch hats headed, I supposed, for their tenement rooms. Ladies passed in fashionable skirts both wide and long. And many a solitary child, grubby and ill-kempt, hurried by, no doubt returning home from their employment too.

These sightings were of everyday things and people,

things that I had observed countless times and had made little of, a mere catalog of city life. That evening, however, I did not see things in my ordinary fashion. That is to say, I saw everything as if it were a photograph: isolated, framed, and distinct. Never before had I been so aware of the city's vitality! It was as if I had new-made eyes. Whether objects or persons, everything was sharp, vivid, intensely alive in the lens of my mind. It was as if I had found a new way of seeing. Was it because I had taken my first photographs?

So transfixed was I by what I observed, I lost myself in simply looking. I don't know how much time I spent, but with a start, I recalled my appointment with Pegg and bolted.

When I finally reached Fifth Avenue, it was all but deserted of pedestrians. Yellow light from house windows fell upon the empty sidewalks as if the whole city were now a darkroom. Now and again a carriage or omnibus clattered by, the *clop-clop* of horse hooves clear and sharp in the night. I was reminded of the ticking grandfather clock in the Von Macht house and its monotonous count toward infinity.

I'm not exactly certain how close to nine o'clock it was when I drew up to the Von Macht house. The windows were dark, but I knew them to be heavily curtained. With luck, the Von Machts had gone out. I could only hope that Pegg would be able to talk to me.

I made my way into the little forecourt and then down

two steps until I stood beneath the stoop. Though the night was dark, I could make out the door. I tapped on it softly.

It opened immediately. Pegg, her face darker in the night, looked out. "Horace?" she whispered.

"It's me."

She grasped my sleeve and pulled me forward. A tiny click informed me she had shut the door. She led me to the scullery door. "The key."

I gave it to her. We went into the room where I had processed the plates. Once inside Pegg locked the door behind us.

Pegg lit a small candle. It burned between us, like some fortune teller's golden orb, as we silently looked at each other. I confess, I wondered whether or not I could trust her. I have no doubt she considered me with the same question. Without doubt, she was taking the greater risk.

Under the pressure of possible discovery, I made myself speak. "Why did you wish me to come?"

She must have caught the nervousness in my voice because she whispered, "Don't worry. The Von Machts are not here."

"Good."

"Please," she said, "I need you to explain the photograph your Mr. Middleditch gave to my mistress."

"Did you see it?

"After you left, Mrs. Von Macht went to her bedroom. I

was able to look at it then. Horace, there was a . . . ghostly image of Eleanora in it."

"Tell me exactly what you saw," I said. She described the angry face.

I considered telling her the truth as I understood it right then, but I held back. "Do you," I asked, "believe it's her ghost?"

"I don't know. But Horace, if she has come back, I've great fears."

"Why?"

"If it *is* Eleanora and she's still angry, she'll do great harm."

I understood perfectly that we were talking about a ghost. Yet the two of us were speaking rationally about something I thought mere superstition. It was as if, having always believed coal was black, I now began to see it as white!

I said, "What do you mean, 'still' angry? I wish you'd tell me more."

"I don't know . . ."

"Pegg, I beg you. I know nothing about her. Or you, really. You said Eleanora was not the Von Machts' real daughter. That they treated her cruelly."

She sighed. "It's a sad story," she said. "And a long one. I don't know when the Von Machts will be back. The moment they return, they'll call for me."

"I can always let myself out," I said, impatient for her to begin.

Pegg was quiet for a moment, then blew out the candle. "The darkness fits the story," she whispered.

"Tell me," I said.

"Eleanora," Pegg began, "was the daughter of Mrs. Von Macht's sister, Chloe. Chloe's husband, Eleanora's father— his name was Tobias Sedgewick—was an Abolitionist, a defender of the Union, and a radical Republican, active in Lincoln's government. His iron mill supplied plate metal for the Union navy's ironclads during the war. It brought him a great fortune. When he died suddenly in the early years of the war, Eleanora and her mother inherited his wealth, more when his business was sold.

"Soon after her husband's death, Mrs. Sedgewick, Eleanora's widowed mother, moved with her daughter to New York City to a house on Park Avenue. They wanted to be nearer to her family. The Von Machts welcomed Chloe and Eleanora, but when Mr. Von Macht tried to take control of their fortune, relations became strained.

"My own parents were escaped slaves, fleeing from the South not long before the war. Noah Longman was my father's name. My mother's was Pegg, like mine. I was born here in the city in 1859, the same year as Eleanora. Shortly after arriving here, my parents died of exhaustion and illness. I was placed in the Colored Orphan Asylum on Fifth and Forty-third Street. That's the asylum that burned down during the riots of 1863, when so many blacks were killed by those protesting against the army draft. So at the age of four I was all alone for a second time.

"Eleanora's mother had the same ideals as her husband, which included believing in equality for all. She took me in. And more than that, she considered me her second daughter. I called her Mama. Eleanora and I, being the same age, were raised together, treated the same, educated equally. We became loving sisters, sharing all, with great tenderness and kindness.

"In our happy days before we came to this house, Eleanora and I loved to dance. She would wear a black dress, I a white one. Pretending to be elves, holding lighted candles and each other's hands, we danced in the dusk like fireflies, laughing all the time.

"Then, in 1870, Mama died in the city's cholera epidemic. We two girls were eleven years old.

"I was orphaned yet again, and since Mama had not finished fully adopting me as her daughter—I had nothing. Eleanora, however, was a very wealthy heiress.

"The Von Machts immediately gathered her up and went so far as to officially adopt her. They hoped to control her wealth and establish more firmly their place in New York society.

"When they took Eleanora, they took me, too. But I was brought along not as a sister but as a servant—an unpaid servant.

"Eleanora was furious about their treatment of me. And she didn't hide her feelings from the Von Machts. For my part I was willing to accept my new role so as not to be separated from my sister. Besides, where else could I have gone?

"Around this time Mr. Von Macht suffered some business reversals. Once again he tried to take hold of Eleanora's wealth. He drew up some papers and asked her to sign them.

"Eleanora, still seething about the way they treated me, refused. She found a way to complain to Dr. Sloper, the family doctor, and to the family lawyer as well. Mrs. Von Macht was enraged, fearing that Eleanora might ruin her position in society.

"That was when Eleanora began to be mistreated. Neglected, punished for trifles, deprived of food. It was all done privately. To the outside world the Von Machts treated Eleanora as their beloved daughter. They claimed she had an illness and could not be seen. In fact, Eleanora was constantly watched, restrained, so she could not seek assistance.

"When she became ill and asked to see the doctor, the Von Machts offered Eleanora treatment only if she would sign the papers. She continued to refuse.

"But she and I," Pegg went on, "held on to our love, supporting each other as only sisters can. Not a day passed that we did not share our mutual misfortunes. Our many embraces were blessed by our loving tears. Eleanora swore she would not abide her mistreatment or mine. It was all one to her.

"We began to suspect that the Von Machts were working toward that day when Eleanora would die—that they might inherit her wealth."

"Didn't you think of running away?"

"We planned to."

"What happened?"

"Eleanora, trying to find someone to help us, told Cook. But Cook, in fear, told Mrs. Von Macht. From then on, Eleanora was confined to that top-floor room.

"I watched as she grew ever weaker and more ill. I pleaded with Mrs. Von Macht to get a doctor. The woman called me terrible names, said Eleanora had only to sign the papers and all would be well.

"Eleanora was not so much stubborn as enraged. She would not yield.

"Did the Von Machts mean to murder her? Perhaps not. But Eleanora and I knew the end was near. I begged her to sign the papers and save her life.

"Then," said Pegg with the utmost solemnity, "she made a sacred vow. She said that when she died she would find a way to come back and wreak her revenge—for the two of us—on the Von Machts.

"In the end she hadn't eaten for ten days. They still refused to get a doctor."

"But . . . they are monsters!" I cried when I'd heard the whole story. "Why didn't they turn on you?"

"Why should they? The lowest servant. I had nothing they wanted. Horace, I think Eleanora died the better to avenge herself."

"Committing suicide?" I cried in dismay.

"I wouldn't call it that," said Pegg. "I think she chose to let go, the better to have her revenge."

"Do you really believe that?" I asked.

Pegg hesitated a moment, then asked, "Was the photograph truly her?"

I hardly knew what to say.

"Horace," she said, grasping my arm, "Eleanora is dead. But I think you've given her a way to come back."

"Me?"

"Those photographs that were taken, they seem to have done it."

"But how?" I said, quite astonished.

"I don't know."

For a moment we were both silent.

"Horace," said Pegg, "do you remember that crack on the photographic plate?"

"I thought you did it. I'm sorry for that."

"I think it was Eleanora."

"What do you mean?" I said.

"Maybe," she said, as if feeling her way in the dark

room, "maybe the crack was like a . . . door. She came from wherever she went, back here . . . that way."

"That can't be!"

"I should so like to see her," whispered Pegg. "To dance with her again."

"Pegg," I asked, "why did Mrs. Von Macht want a photograph?"

"These days Mrs. Von Macht's friends talk a great deal about spirits. The talk worried Mrs. Von Macht. She decided to put her photograph on Eleanora's tomb to scare Eleanora's spirit away—just in case. She told me to find an unknown photographer, so none of her friends would know what she was doing."

"And the candlestick," I asked, "why is that in the pictures?"

"It was the first thing Mrs. Von Macht purchased after Eleanora died. She wanted it in the pictures to mock Eleanora, to remind her of her defeat. Horace, since the Von Machts took possession of Eleanora's money, not a day has passed without some extravagant purchase."

"Why did she say she had many pictures of Eleanora?"

"She'll say anything to make people believe she cared for her."

What could I say to such crimes? Such a recital was its own condemnation.

"Horace," said Pegg, "you should be going. The Von Machts may come home."

I was reluctant to leave. "Pegg," I said, "we must talk more."

"I'll find a way," she said, taking my hand and leading me from the dark room out to the hallway and back to the door. When we reached the doorway, we stood there for a moment, hands clasped. I didn't wish to leave her and I think she did not want me to go. But of course, I had to.

Within moments I stood beneath the dark stoop, the door to the Von Macht house closed behind me. As I walked back to our rooms, I reviewed Pegg's story. A ghastly tale. If ever a spirit had reason to seek revenge, Eleanora had it. Yet true reason said such a thing could not be done!

Reaching home, I was glad that Mr. Middleditch hadn't returned. No doubt he was still celebrating his fraud. I got ready for bed.

But as I was removing my jacket, I came upon the print of the four images I had taken to Pegg. I had become so absorbed in her story, I had forgotten to share it with her. I pulled it out but suddenly found myself reluctant to look at it. Next moment, I chided myself for being so foolish and made myself look.

It was like a blow to my heart: For what I saw on that print were not four images of Eleanora Von Macht but *five*.

I stared with disbelieving eyes. I had done no more than carry the print in my pocket. But there it was, as if self-created, another image of Eleanora Von Macht—and the clearest yet.

In the end I decided what I was seeing was not there, because it could not be. I made up my mind that it was simply a nightmare, a fixation concocted in my tired brain.

Slipping out of my clothes, I blew out the candle, buried myself under the blankets, and tried to convince myself that in the morning I'd wake from this dream and the ghostly fifth face would be gone.

Unable to sleep, a new thought came: Each new image of Eleanora was in better focus. It was as if my presence brought the face into the photograph—as if the ghost of Eleanora was coming closer and closer to this world!

Was Pegg right? Had I somehow brought her back into life?

TWENTY-ONE

I MUST HAVE FALLEN ASLEEP at last. When I woke next morning, the first thing I did was snatch up the print and look for that fifth image.

It had vanished.

Enormously relieved, I told myself that it had been a dream after all. In fact, I was quite prepared to consider everything I thought I had seen and done a bad dream. Of course, when I checked the photograph, those four images remained. No matter. The fifth image did not exist, and for the moment that was enough. It enabled me to put aside my irrational ideas of ghosts. My old sense of reason reasserted itself. I had no doubt I would find an explanation for the rest. And yet . . . and yet . . . it wasn't long before my unease returned.

Mr. Middleditch soon arose. He was still feeling very chipper, and over our usual breakfast of oatmeal and coffee he insisted upon regaling me with an account of the good time he had enjoyed the night before. His mood was so jaunty I ventured to ask, "Were you bragging about what you did?"

"Me?" he cried with a guffaw. "Brag about the spirit photography business? I should hope not. I might as well run an advertisement in the *Daily News* to tell other photographers how they could horn in on my business. But Horace, I've been thinking how we should prepare for the next round."

"What next round?"

"Mrs. Von Macht will call us back."

"How can you be so sure?"

"You'll see," he said with a grin. "She'll want another photograph, the better to determine if what she saw was a fluke." He laughed. "I intend to be prepared."

"In what way?"

"She'll ask me about the image. I'll remind her that when she first visited me at my studio she spoke of souls, or ghosts, and . . . what was it? Ectoplasm. That she felt her late daughter was restless. Something like that. I'll remind her that it was she who had to convince me there was an image among the palms. And that's not all."

"What do you mean?"

"I've decided we should go to the cemetery—Brooklyn's

Green-Wood Cemetery. Photograph that poor girl's grave."

"Why?"

"I'll tell Mrs. Von Macht I was so touched by her story—by her deep-felt grief—that I was moved to visit the girl's resting place. What's more, I felt absolutely compelled to photograph it. And *voilà*! Another spirit photograph."

"But—"

"We'll use the spy camera—the more practiced we are, the better."

Of course, he said *we*, but I knew perfectly well he meant *me*. "Must I?" I said.

He laughed. "Now, Horace, am I not your devoted teacher? And you, my loyal apprentice? So of course you must go. And since it's a long way, you'd better get started."

With much reluctance I did so.

The sky was dull that morning, the air chilly with a feel of impending rain. I was glad I had my coat, though the jostling spy camera was a bother.

All the same, I traveled to the bottom of Manhattan and paid two pennies for the South Ferry across the crowded East River to the city of Brooklyn. Once there I boarded one of the plodding omnibuses that ran directly to the cemetery, some two and a half miles away. I left Charlton Street at about nine in the morning and did not arrive at the cemetery gates until near one in the afternoon.

Green-Wood Cemetery was not an ordinary graveyard,

nor just a burial ground for the wealthy and fashionable. No, Green-Wood was and is where people of great renown and importance are buried. (My namesake, Horace Greeley, had recently been laid to rest there.) Moreover, thousands of people visit its vastness—not only to see the graves of the famous, but also to see elegant sculpture and, I dare say, to enjoy the clean Brooklyn air, so different from Manhattan's.

The main gates are like some fantastical beachside sand castle with three gothic towers that stand more than a hundred feet tall. The massive structure is adorned with countless arches, battlements, towers, gables, and religious carvings. Resurrection is the theme, and the gates are emblazoned with sayings such as "The Dead Shall Be Reborn."

Flanking the twin entry gates are offices. Within the right-hand one, I found a uniformed guard—a Gettysburg veteran with one arm and a spread of medals on his chest. He was seated behind a desk covered with large ledgers.

"Help you, young man?"

I informed him that I was visiting a grave.

"Which family?"

"Von Macht."

"Ah! Yes, indeed. That sad affair. The parents quite cut up. But," he said, looking up and cocking an eyebrow, "it didn't prevent them from holding a very fashionable entombment."

He opened a ledger, wet his thumb with his tongue, and flipped through pages, fingering the columns until he announced, "Von Macht. Lot Eighty-two." He pointed to an elaborate wall map depicting many paths as intertwined as a dish of noodles. The Von Macht mausoleum, he indicated, was on Rue Path. He was kind enough to draw a map.

"Best hurry," he warned. "Storm's coming."

I set off.

Map in hand, I walked along the ways (Sunset Path, Sylvan Avenue) through the cemetery's vast sculpture garden of gray, stone-hewed grief. It was exceedingly hilly and irregular. Within its valleys I could see little save brown grass, leafless trees, grave markers, and mausoleums. At the highest elevations I could observe Manhattan; the Lower Bay, full of ships; and even New Jersey.

Closer at hand were graves by the hundreds—a city of the dead, populated by weeping stone gods, goddesses, saints, animals, and angels. Everywhere images of deceased persons were on display, usually in small frames. A few were photographs.

While some graves were pathetically small, for infants, others were showy, large enough for whole genealogies to gather within. A fair number had massive entryways with stone sheep, lions, and even a sleeping dragon for eternal guardians. Some graves were embedded in the hillsides.

The day's light being dreary, and as there was no true

greenery, the only bright color was the occasional discarded or decaying flower. It made me feel as if I were drifting through a garden of shadows—as if I had entered into a living photograph.

It being a weekday and the weather increasingly threatening, only a few people were about, mostly mourning families with children. So as I wended my way along the twisted paths, I was for the most part a solitary wanderer. By the time I stood before the Von Macht tomb, thunder was rumbling.

The tomb was a grandiose stone structure with a pair of large iron doors. Over the door's lintel was carved the name VON MACHT. Above stood a statue of God in glory, His arms spread wide as if grateful to receive the Von Machts. His feet trampled a vanquished stone skeleton—a symbol of death, I supposed. The skull leered as if mocking me. It fleetingly occurred to me that its expression was that of the photographed face of Eleanora.

On one of the doors a stone tablet listed the names of those interred, the last one freshly chiseled: ELEANORA. I gazed upon the doors, and wondered what lay beyond, if the poor girl truly rested easy.

Right next to the tomb, a little bit apart, was a figure that caught my attention: a tall, gray, and beautiful angel, her great wings drooping, her head slightly bowed in deep-felt sorrow, grief personified. For a moment I was sure she was weeping, but then realized the tears were rain, which had begun to fall.

I stepped back, and since no one was about, made no attempt to conceal that I took six hurried photographs, the maximum allowed on the camera's circular plate.

With the rain now increasing steadily, I was glad to turn back. But I had gone only a few paces when a crack of lightning burst above. In the flash of white light I spied a young girl in a black dress dart across the gap between two tombs. Having been lost in thought, to see her dash by was startling. Moreover, such was my constant preoccupation that for a second I actually thought the girl was Eleanora.

I stood stock still, my legs shaky, my heart pounding almost (I'm sure) as loudly as the storm's thunder. But the girl was gone as quickly as the lightning, presumably over a hill and thus lost to sight.

I took a deep breath and began to flee the pelting storm, all the while trying to convince myself that I had not seen what I saw.

The journey home was cold, dull, and damp, my thoughts filled with much foreboding.

TWENTY-TWO

I REACHED OUR ROOMS close to seven o'clock. Upon arriving, I found a note from Mr. Middleditch: *"Went out."*

Glad to be alone, I got out of my wet clothes, devoured a simple supper of bread, cheese, and a bumper of tepid milk. I told myself that in the morning I would get up early and develop my new pictures. Though it was not late, I went to bed—the sooner to rise.

Again, I could not sleep. In my mind, I kept wandering through Green-Wood Cemetery—seeing it as a photograph. I saw anew the countless graves. The tall, gray, grieving angel. The storm. I recalled the briefly noticed girl—in her black dress. But no matter how I twisted and turned (in body and thought), I always seemed to return to the Von Macht tomb—as if it were pulling at my thoughts, at me.

Accepting that sleep was not possible, I got up and decided I might as well develop the pictures I'd taken. And after going through the usual process, I eventually had a decent negative—six pictures—all of the tomb. Using a magnifying glass, I held it up to the candlelight.

I gasped. The fragile glass plate nearly slipped from my fingers. For in indistinct but undeniable fashion, there were not just pictures of the tomb but images of Eleanora Von Macht! Not just her face, but her full self—in a black frock.

As for the sorrowful angel, she was not in my pictures. She had vanished from the scene.

I noticed another thing: As I had first observed of the images from the Von Macht house, the focus on each image of Eleanora became progressively sharper, so that the last image was as real as life.

I stood there in great distress. My head fairly seethed. My jaw clenched. I wanted to cry. The next moment my mind went to the words on the cemetery gate: The Dead Shall Be Reborn. In that moment my understanding of the world completely altered. My body turned cold. Tears ran down my face as I had to accept the extraordinary fact: I, Horace Carpetine, had somehow brought Eleanora Von Macht back into the living world.

TWENTY-THREE

"D ID YOU GET SOME DECENT pictures of the girl's grave?"
Mr. Middleditch asked over breakfast next morning.

I was hardly able to answer. I had slept little. I was tense, and quite upset. The considerable time I'd spent thinking how I was to answer his inevitable question had brought little comfort.

"I did," I said. "But . . ."

"But what?"

"Something happened to ruin them."

"Ruin them? Do you mean to say you've already made prints?"

"Just negatives."

"What's the problem, then?"

"I don't know how it happened. I was concentrating so on

taking the pictures that . . . someone got into them."

He wagged a finger at me. "That, young Horace, is the classic photographer's botch!"

"I'm . . . sorry."

"Oh, well. You can always go back. But better show them to me. Perhaps they can be salvaged."

I fetched the negatives. Squinting, he held them up to the light. "Fetch the magnifying lens."

I did.

He looked and said, "Is that a girl standing there?"

"I think so."

"Mean-spirited little tyke," he said, not realizing who it was. "And you didn't notice?"

"No, sir," I answered truthfully.

"Any idea who?"

"A ghost."

He laughed. "You really are getting into the spirit of things, aren't you?" he said with a grin. "Ah, well, consider it practice. You will need to go back. Let's just be patient. I suspect we'll hear from Mrs. Von Macht before too long."

He was right. Next day a message came by post:

> *Mr. Middleditch: Would you be kind*
> *enough to call at my home at 3 p.m.*
> *I shall send my carriage for you.*
> MRS. FREDERICK VON MACHT

Needless to say, Mr. Middleditch was elated by what he took as a request. I saw it as a summons.

"Shall I come?" I asked.

"By all means, Horace. You're very much a part of all this. You must have your enjoyment, too."

That was fine with me. I needed to see Pegg again, to continue our conversation, and to tell her what had happened at the cemetery.

Later that day—Mr. Middleditch didn't notice—I quietly made two prints of one of my photographs of the Von Macht tomb. I intended to give one to Pegg.

Next afternoon at two thirty the Von Macht carriage came to our door, and we were taken to the Fifth Avenue house. Pegg let us in. When she did, she and I exchanged knowing looks, nothing more. She led the way to the parlor, holding the door open. Since Mr. Middleditch entered before me, I was able to slip my photograph to Pegg without anyone noticing. She took it and shut the door behind us.

Mrs. Von Macht was as elegant as ever, in a dark purple dress, quite striking against her black hair. In her hands was the photograph Mr. Middleditch had made. She seemed tense.

She was not alone. Her husband was with her. When I had first seen him, he had appeared angry. Now he stood red-faced, jaw muscles pulsating, a clenched fist gripping a walking stick as if about to give way to outright violence.

Alarmed, I took my place behind Mr. Middleditch, a little off to one side.

"Mr. Middleditch," said the woman, "so kind of you to come."

He made his little bow. "Mrs. Von Macht. Mr. Von Macht. How can I be of service?" he said.

"Sir," Mr. Von Macht cried with great force. "How do you explain this . . . photograph?" He gestured toward the image in his wife's hands.

Mr. Middleditch appeared taken aback. "Sir?" he managed to say.

"Mr. Middleditch," said the woman in more controlled tones, "what my husband is requesting is an understanding of the picture. Some way of knowing how, and why, it contains the face of our late, much mourned daughter, Eleanora."

Mr. Middleditch relaxed. "You'll forgive me, madam," he said. "If I may remind you, it was you who had to convince me it was there."

"Claptrap!" barked Mr. Von Macht, his face turning quite red. "Of course it's there. I presume you aren't blind. Since you're the photographer, I should like to know how it got there."

"It's a mystery to me, sir."

"Mystery!" shouted Mr. Von Macht. "Are you suggesting that it got there of its own accord? Do you take me for a fool, sir?" He shifted his hold on his walking stick menacingly.

"Frederick . . . please!" cried Mrs. Von Macht.

"Never mind, *please*!" Frederick went on, taking two steps toward Mr. Middleditch, his stick twitching in his hand. "Sir, you are asked to take a photograph of my wife. You do. But when you present it to her, there, lurking in the background is the face of our dead daughter. I insist upon an explanation. How did it get there?"

Mr. Middleditch was remarkably unflustered. "I can only recall madam's words when she first visited me at my studio," he said, smooth as velvet. "Remember, madam? You had heard it said that souls, or ghosts—or I think you used the word 'ectoplasm'—of the deceased linger. And that you, madam, felt your late daughter was restless. You did say something of the sort, did you not?"

"I suppose I did," the woman admitted under her husband's withering glance.

"Then perhaps," suggested Mr. Middleditch, "your daughter hovers closer than you think. Perhaps my photograph has merely captured that . . . lingering."

"Is that the best you can do?" sneered Mr. Von Macht.

"I suppose," Mr. Middleditch said, "my camera—or I—could be . . . extra sensitive."

This was so smoothly offered that only silence ensued. Mr. Von Macht, his pointed beard and florid face giving him a devilish cast, did not seem to know what else to say or—happily—to do.

As for Mrs. Von Macht, she simply gazed upon the photograph.

At last Mr. Middleditch said, "Is there any reason why her soul should be restless?"

Mr. Middleditch, having none of the knowledge I had, asked the question in complete innocence. The result: Mrs. Von Macht bolted up from the sofa and stood by the curtained window, her back to us. As for Mr. Von Macht, the color drained from his normally red face. He even lifted his walking stick so that I was sure he would strike Mr. Middleditch. Instead, he flung it away, smashing a piece of pottery.

Mr. Middleditch, in his bulldog manner, apparently taking no notice of what he had provoked, went blithely on. "I have, perhaps, a suggestion."

"Which is?" Mr. Von Macht managed to say.

"Allow me to take another photograph. With the same camera, of course. Perhaps the first was just an . . . aberration. A . . . mistake. An odd . . . configuration."

"And I suppose," sneered Mr. Von Macht, "you would charge us for more photographs?"

"It does, as madam has witnessed, take time, and—"

"Yes, do it!" cried Mrs. Von Macht. "I must see another picture. I don't care about cost. And the sooner, the better." She went over to the sofa, picked up the picture Mr. Middleditch had first made, and tore it up into bits. "This has caused much pain." She scattered the pieces.

Even as she did so, I saw Eleanora's mocking face behind her. It was all I could do not to cry out. For the face now had absolute clarity, as if it were truly *there,* a living presence. I dared not say a word.

"I'm so sorry," murmured Mr. Middleditch. "When shall we return?"

"Never," barked Mr. Von Macht.

"Mr. Middleditch shall come back tomorrow," said Mrs. Von Macht, as much to her husband as to the photographer.

"Olivia!" the man cried. "Leave it alone!"

"I must know if it's her," the woman replied.

Mr. Von Macht looked around for his walking stick, snatched it, and shouted, "You are a fool!" That said, he whirled about and sped from the room, slamming the door behind him.

Mrs. Von Macht stood so still, it was as if every part of her body were struggling for self-control.

Mr. Middleditch went on as if these were normal events. "As you wish, madam. Tomorrow. My boy can make arrangements this very afternoon. "

"It will have to be this evening," Mrs. Von Macht spoke with effort. "I'm giving a tea at four."

"Whatever you desire," said Mr. Middleditch. He turned to me. "Horace . . ." He gestured toward the door.

I sprang to open it.

Pegg was in the hallway. Whether she had heard anything

of what transpired, I could not tell. Her face revealed nothing.

She led the way out. At the door I said to her, "I'll be coming back this evening. Mrs. Von Macht wishes another photographic session. I'll need to set things up."

"I'll be here to help you, sir," Pegg returned without visible emotion. Her eyes, however, spoke of complete understanding. For the first time I saw real fright in her face.

TWENTY-FOUR

Though the Von Macht carriage was waiting to take us home, Mr. Middleditch suggested that we walk. I knew why. The man was jubilant.

"Oh, Horace!" he cried after we'd walked a few blocks. "Am I not an absolute genius?" He clapped me on the back.

I, of course, had very different thoughts. I was thinking Mr. Middleditch had best be careful. Mr. Von Macht was clearly capable of violence, and his wife was greatly distraught. If either of them discovered Mr. Middleditch's hoax, things might go very badly. And what, I wondered, would they do if they discovered that Eleanora's ghost was real?

Still, one thing Mr. Middleditch had said caused me to consider a last notion in respect to my responsibility in these events. It involved the camera. In search of an explanation for what was happening that did not implicate me, I needed to check it. After all, it had been the Stirn Concealed Vest Camera with which I'd taken all the pictures of Eleanora. Perhaps it was the camera, not me, that brought the girl back.

I recalled that on the camera was a little brass plate that indicated where Mr. Middleditch had made his purchase. When we returned to our rooms, I went to it and looked at the address anew.

JOHN STOCK & CO.

PHOTOGRAPHIC MATERIALS

NO. 2 RIVINGTON STREET

NEAR THE BOWERY

There being some hours before I had to return to the Von Macht house, I made up my mind to go.

Mr. Middleditch was lounging in our front reception room, reading the *Daily News*.

"Mr. Middleditch, sir," I began. "I was thinking."

"Ah! Solemn Horace! You do too much of that," he returned from behind the paper, laughing, as always, at his own joke.

"We only had two plates for the spy camera. Don't you think we should get more?"

"Good idea."

"I'd be happy to fetch a few."

"Excellent. You're full of industry, Horace."

He gave me some cash to purchase the plates, and I wrote

down the name and address of the dealer.

As it turned out, John Stock & Co. was a small shop, selling a variety of cameras and photographic apparatus, chemicals, papers, and equipment. The proprietor, Mr. Stock, a white-haired old man who spoke with a thick German accent, was perfectly friendly. Indeed, in the course of our conversation, when I told him my father was in the watch repair trade, he acted as if I were some kind of relation—the love of mechanical things, I suppose—and was even more welcoming.

I purchased the circular plates, explaining I was apprenticed to Mr. Middleditch, the photographer. Then I asked Mr. Stock if anyone had ever reported anything unusual about the spy camera.

"Unusual? In what way?"

"Distortions. Odd focus. Anything not straightforward. Double images."

"*Ja,*" he said, "it's awkward to use that camera in—what do you say—hiding. But no, absolutely nothing such as you speak. Do you have it with you?"

I gave it to him and he examined it closely, inside and out.

"In perfection," Mr. Stock announced. "Same as others."

I had not expected a different answer. This is to say, my own logic insisted that in some extraordinary way, it was I, and only I, who was responsible for bringing Eleanora back.

The notion filled me with horror—and fear for what might yet occur.

TWENTY-FIVE

EARLY THAT EVENING I took a carriage to the Von Machts' house to bring our equipment. Though Mr. Middleditch was willing to pay the cab hire, he said—it was his laziness, I'm sure—that he could not be bothered to go.

"You know what to do as well as I," he allowed. "But I suggest you seek out that colored girl. She may be wobbly in her head, but she should be able to help you find some more images of that dead girl. I promise: They will be somewhere."

I gritted my teeth and just went.

It was dark when I reached the house and entered through the main door. Pegg unlocked it and led me right to the scullery. As soon as we got inside, we shut the door like two conspirators. Which I suppose we were.

"Did you look at that cemetery picture?" was the first thing I asked. She nodded. "Was it Eleanora?"

"I think so. Horace, why did you even go there?"

I had already resolved to tell Pegg everything about Mr. Middleditch's swindle for three reasons: First, I was embarrassed by his scheme and didn't wish to be associated with it. Second, I was repulsed by his demeaning talk about Pegg. I had no doubt who was my true friend. Last, and perhaps most important, I needed greater understanding about what was happening regarding Eleanora's ghost. So as I set out our equipment, I talked.

I told Pegg all, right from the beginning, and she listened intently.

When I'd finished, she was silent a long while. "Then the picture Mr. Middleditch gave Mrs. Von Macht was . . . false," she said, her voice full of anger. "And you were willing to trick me, too."

"Yes . . . and no."

"How both?" she demanded.

"The picture he made is false. But . . . Eleanora's face in that picture is not the one he put in. Pegg, it's real."

"How did it get there?"

"I don't know!"

She held up the cemetery picture. "And this?"

"I took that picture. But Pegg," I pleaded, "believe me. I didn't put Eleanora in it. She just . . . appeared. And there's another thing. As I was leaving the Von Macht tomb, I saw . . . her."

"Saw her!" she cried.

136

I described my sighting, how, in the brief burst of lightning, I was sure I'd seen her run by. "She was wearing a black dress."

"She was buried in a black dress," said Pegg, her anger melting in remembrance. "I dressed her. It was her favorite. Her dancing dress."

"Pegg, forgive me, but . . . but are you quite certain she . . . died?"

She didn't flinch from the question. "I was holding her hand when she took her last breath."

"Pegg, you told me Eleanora talked to you."

She smiled sadly. "I knew her so well I've only to think about something and it's as if I hear her voice speaking to me in my head."

"But not," I asked with care, "as if anyone else—such as me—might hear?"

"Of course not." She sighed. "Oh, Horace, I do wish I could see her."

"But since she died, you've never seen her?"

"Only in your pictures."

"Pegg," I said, "I don't understand how she's come to be in them."

She was quiet for a moment. "I've thought about it a great deal," she said. "Perhaps when you take your pictures—the more you take, the more you draw her forth."

That Pegg should say what I had only dared think made me tremble. "But . . . how could that be?" I asked.

Again Pegg was still. But at length she said, "Before Mama

died—in our happy days—Eleanora and I were given many books to read. One book I read told about ancient days when there were seers."

"Seers?"

"Wise people who saw things no one else could. Maybe you're like that."

"Pegg," I protested, "I'm not wise."

"Did you take many pictures before?"

"The first pictures I ever took were with that spy camera—those pictures of Eleanora."

"Horace, I think when you take pictures you become a seer. Your pictures draw Eleanora forth."

The notion seemed utterly fantastic. And yet— "If I have," I said, almost afraid to speak, "as you say, drawn her forth, what do you think . . . she'll do?"

"She'll take her revenge on Mr. and Mrs. Von Macht."

"In what . . . way?"

"I think she will kill them."

There it was, the very thought I'd kept hidden from myself, even as I knew it was within me: Eleanora was bent on murdering the Von Machts. I had to swallow before I could say, "And I'm the one . . . who will have made it possible for her to do so. Is that . . . right?"

The look Pegg bestowed upon me was not of awe, not of revulsion, but of pity. Tears were in her eyes. I shall be ever grateful to her for that. As for my question, she did not reply. No matter. I knew the answer for myself.

"Pegg," I whispered, "do you wish the Von Machts to be . . . killed?"

She smeared her tears away and pondered my question a long while. "Horace," she finally said, "when people burned down the colored orphanage . . ." She shuddered visibly. "Horace, I've seen so many killed. So much suffering. I'll never forget it. I do want to see the Von Machts punished for what they've done. But no, not . . . murdered."

"But if Eleanora has come back and means to kill them," I pleaded, "what are we to do?"

A gong rang from somewhere in the house.

She bolted up. "The Von Machts are back," she whispered. "It's later than I realized. You shouldn't still be here."

"I was supposed to set things up," I reminded her. "Anyway, I can wait a bit and then let myself out through the servants' door."

She went to the scullery door only to hesitate. "Horace," she whispered, "if I could just speak to Eleanora, I'd tell her that she should rest in peace. That I'm fine. That I will never stop loving her."

"Perhaps that would help," I said. "Now go. I'll lock the door behind you. We'll talk more tomorrow."

She opened the door, only to pause at the threshold. "Horace!" she whispered, "I'm glad you're my friend." She darted back, gave me a hug, and then ran off.

I was alone.

TWENTY-SIX

I RELOCKED THE DOOR and sat against the wall. I kept thinking about Pegg's notion that I was what she called a seer. It was such an extraordinary idea, I found it difficult to accept. Instead, I reviewed all that had happened, trying to do so in the most logical, rational of ways.

One: When I took the pictures, they contained images of the spirit world.

Two: The very act of my taking pictures drew these spirits back to the real world.

Three: The more pictures I took, the more real they became.

Finally: When real enough, they became independent of me—which is to say, they became living ghosts.

It was like the process of developing a photograph I have described:

as if the shadow were coming from some mystic depth, emerging from another world, taking, little by little, bodily shape and form until that shadow becomes . . . real.

Exactly what I'd done for Eleanora's spirit!

The facts of the matter were perfectly clear—though surely not normal. My picture taking had summoned a ghost, and not just any ghost, but one bent on murder!

I could argue with myself—did argue!—that the Von Machts were frightful people who deserved punishment. But if Pegg—with all her suffering—chose compassion, could I choose anything less?

By now the house had grown absolutely still. Enough time had passed. I needed to get out.

I peered out the front window to make sure the carriage was not at the curb. It was not. I made my way, fumbling but quiet, out of the scullery and down the dark hallway to the front door and its handle.

It was locked.

For that door I had no key.

TWENTY-SEVEN

TAKEN BY SURPRISE, I RETREATED in haste to the scullery, shut the door, locked it, sat on the floor, and pulled my knees up, as if being small would keep me from being discovered.

Not that anyone came. There was nothing but darkness, the quiet, and me, along with a slight whiff of my photographic chemicals hovering in the air. For a while I entertained the notion that Pegg would return. But there was no reason for her to do so. On the contrary, she had every reason to assume I had gone.

So I continued to sit there in the deep stillness.

From time to time I heard a few noises from above, rather like steps, or so I supposed. These sounds did not last very long, and then the house folded back into silence.

I kept telling myself I could not stay. It was too danger-ous. Pegg and I were in a difficult enough situation. If I were to be found, it could only make things much worse.

Then I remembered: When Mr. Middleditch and I first came to the house, Pegg had opened the main door using a key. She had set that key on a little table right by the door. Perhaps it was always kept there. But though that key was the only hope for escape, I knew I must not try for it as long as there was the slightest suggestion of anyone moving about upstairs.

Finally, having heard nothing for what seemed a great while, I mustered my courage, opened the door carefully, stepped into the hall, and paused to listen. Nothing. I reached the steps and went up slowly, always looking about, always listening. Gradually, my eyes became accustomed to the gloom.

I reached the first floor and stood at the back of the large hallway. Neither the gas chandelier nor the wall sconces were lit. Though I could not see the lofty ceilings, I sensed them. As for sound, all I heard was the grandfather clock tick-tocking, tick-tocking, tick-tocking.

Far down the hallway I could make out, past the stairway, the front door. I could also just see the little side table. Whether the key was on it I could not tell.

Knowing I must move to get out, I took a deep breath and commenced creeping down the hallway. The carpeted floors muffled my steps. Even so, I hadn't gone more than a few steps before I had to stop. I was panting so, I felt faint. I forced myself to stand still and breathe deeply. All the while I listened. The house felt cold and hollow around me, much what I imagined it must feel like inside the Von Machts' Green-Wood tomb.

Regaining my composure, I continued to creep forward, my eyes focused not so much on the door but on that little table, hoping with real desperation that the key would be there.

A few more steps and I saw something of the table's surface. A little farther on, relief swept through me. The key was there.

When I was close enough to the table, I reached out and picked up the key in my shaky hand, then moved closer to the door. Even as I touched it, I heard a sound coming from behind me. I started, and looked back.

The door of one of the side rooms slowly opened. Light behind it bloomed. But the open door hid the figure behind it.

If I had had my full wits about me, I would have unlocked the front door and fled. But I was so frightened, I stood frozen.

The first thing to appear from behind the hall door was Mrs. Von Macht's three-pronged silver candlestick. Its candles were lit, the flames fluttering as if caught in a breeze. A shadowy figure followed, small, indistinct, moving noiselessly, effortlessly toward the main stairwell.

Gradually I perceived long, fair hair and a black dress teased by the same currents that fluttered the candle flames. Before me was a girl, barefoot, very thin, arms almost twiglike, so that her dress hung limply.

It was Eleanora Von Macht.

She reached the stairway and began to climb. Halfway up the steps she stopped, and to my horror set the candlestick against the wall. She was going to set the house on fire!

In that instant I recalled that Pegg must be on the third floor. And of course the Von Machts were in their rooms. Before I could consider what I was doing, I cried: "Stop!"

Eleanora whirled about and looked right at me. Oh, the wicked, hateful grin upon her thin, hollow-cheeked face! The next second she vanished, taking the flames with her.

My shout must have woken someone. From above, I heard a door open and slam, then hurried footsteps. I spun about, fitted the key to the front door lock, yanked the door open, threw the key down, and fled.

TWENTY-EIGHT

I RAN SOUTH FOR MANY BLOCKS, until I had to stop to regain my breath. My head was awhirl. If I'd not been there, Eleanora would have set fire to the house. Eleanora! I could hardly believe that I had seen her! But not only had I seen her: I saw how full she was of murderous intent.

Shivering with cold and my own tension, I walked on, glad that it was dark. I didn't want to be seen, consumed by the bizarre notion that anyone who saw me would know what horror I had beheld.

What next? I had to make a test of what Pegg had called my powers as a seer. I must take a photograph of someone not connected to the Von Machts. I considered my family, but decided that would take too long. Then I realized it would be easy to photograph Mr. Middleditch. Surely that would answer my question.

I was caught up in my plans for this experiment when I heard shouts of "Fire! Fire!" The next moment a crowd—boys as always leading the way—was running down Bleecker Street. I looked up, and while I could see nothing but people, I could smell smoke.

After what I had just witnessed, the thought of fire anywhere filled me with the greatest apprehension. I quickened my pace.

By the time I reached the site, a large crowd, mostly men and boys, had gathered to watch. Teams of firemen began to arrive, running alongside the horse teams that pulled the pumpers. These pumpers carried primed steam engines ready to push water through hoses. The firemen, twelve to each pumper, quickly put their hoses to use, working to keep the furious flames from spreading.

As the fire roared, the excited crowd rippled with talk of people who might be trapped within. No one knew if there were any.

City policemen in their dark blue uniforms and caps soon appeared and used their wooden batons to keep the boisterous crowd in order. I squirmed and pushed my way through to the front lines, receiving little buffeting for my efforts.

Once in front of the crowd, I saw that the fire was consuming a large wooden warehouse. The air was filled with a ghastly stench.

Then I saw a long, newly made sign atop the building that provided the name of the business.

F. Von Macht—Trader in Fish

It was already smoldering. Even as I looked on, there was a great *Whoosh!* as a ball of flame erupted. With it came a hideous scream from within the burning building. Simultaneously, I saw Eleanora Von Macht in the fire's midst. In one hand she clutched the Von Machts' three-pronged candlestick. The features of her face were twisted with a terrible, hateful glee!

Stunned, I turned to see if anyone else had seen what I had. It surely did not seem so.

The next moment the entire structure collapsed. The large crowd let forth a collective moan of despair as—on the evidence of the scream—it was thought that a grisly death had occurred. All delight vanished. Now tragedy had been witnessed.

Did the scream proclaim the death of some innocent? Was it Eleanora's cry of wickedness? I never knew. What I did know was that I was terrified. I bolted through the crowd and sped away toward our rooms where, as you might guess, I slept but poorly. My thoughts were churning upon the ghastly events of the night, tormented by dread of what might yet happen.

TWENTY-NINE

A<small>T THE BREAKFAST TABLE</small> Mr. Middleditch asked, "Is everything ready at the Von Machts'?"

"Yes, sir," I replied, not about to tell Mr. Middleditch one word of what I had seen and experienced.

"Did that colored girl tell you where you can find more pictures of Eleanora Von Macht?"

Willing to tell him anything to ensure my continued presence at the Von Macht house, or should I say near Pegg, I answered, "I think I can get more."

"Excellent."

"Sir," I ventured, "would you mind very much if I . . . practiced some picture taking? We have some hours to spare, and I really haven't had that much time with any camera."

"Now that you've started taking pictures, it's an excellent idea."

"Perhaps," I said, "I could take a couple of pictures of you."

"If you'd like."

Which is exactly what I did, taking three pictures after posing him on our receiving room sofa. What's more, I did not use the spy camera.

He was, as I had hoped, quite uninterested.

"If you don't mind, I'll develop them now," I announced, all but numb with foreboding.

"Suit yourself," he returned, already absorbed in his newspaper.

I repaired to our studio and went through the usual preparations. It wasn't long before I was bent over the developing tray, watching images emerge.

Mr. Middleditch's face rose up with considerable clarity, his handlebar mustache distinctive in the negative. But there, hovering over his left shoulder, was a vague image—the face of an elderly man. He was dour, full-bearded, bleakly staring straight out at me. I gazed at this face of the old man even as his dejected, staring eyes held me. These eyes were full of hard sorrow and seemed to come from a great distance.

I did not have the slightest doubt that it was a ghost.

With a sinking heart I deliberately let the plates remain in the developing bath long enough to be sure that both Mr. Middleditch's face and the ghostly image dissolved into darkness.

There was but one thing left to determine, and the occasion for it came over lunch when Mr. Middleditch asked me if I was planning to have dinner with my family the coming weekend.

"I hope so, sir."

"Family is a good thing," he said blithely.

"Mine surely is," I said.

"Lucky you," said Mr. Middleditch.

I took the opportunity. "Sir, may I ask, what was your father like?"

"Oh, him?" he replied, laughing. "The old duffer . . . I fear he and I didn't get along as well as we should have. Always accusing me of being lazy. Hard-faced old skinner, with rather a bleak stare about him. Sorrowful, too. Never laughed. Rarely smiled. Not like me at all."

"Full-bearded?"

"How did you guess?"

I shrugged, hoping I was masking my despair.

"No," continued Mr. Middleditch, "I shouldn't like to have him hovering over my shoulder."

Greatly disturbed, I asked to be excused and took a walk around the block to think. I walked slowly, breathing deeply. It was chilly, but I was sweating. How glad I was I'd let the images vanish!

Pegg was right. I was what she had chosen to call a seer. A seer of shadows. And if my experience with Eleanora was true, there was something much more. I knew, for example, that if I continued to take more pictures of Mr. Middleditch, I would bring his dead father's ghost to life. Not as a living person, but as a freed ghost.

Indeed, I was sure if I took pictures of anyone, I would bring forth shadows of the departed. Could there be anything more astounding—or disturbing? I, a seer of shadows!

And what did it mean for me? What was I supposed to do with this . . . ability? Surely it was a curse!

My emotions quickly gave way to something even more urgent: What were Pegg and I to do about the ghost of Eleanora Von Macht? For I had no doubt that the spirit I had brought back to this world was determined upon murder.

THIRTY

I T WAS TIME TO GO to the Von Macht house.

Before we left, Mr. Middleditch laid out what he assured me would happen. While he took more photographs of Mrs. Von Macht, I would use the spy camera to find and take more pictures of the girl. He then would construct another spirit photograph. "One more spirit photograph," he predicted, "and they will be completely taken in."

"Sir, aren't we taking a great risk?"

"It went smoothly before, didn't it?" he countered.

The best I could reply was "I think Mr. Von Macht is suspicious."

"That type is suspicious of his own shadow. Anyway, I doubt he'll even be there. He doesn't like me. In these matters it's the woman who counts. Our only need is that you get some more images of that dead girl."

My thought was: *I've already taken too many.*

In due time the carriage came, and we set off, the spy camera once more hidden beneath my coat.

When we arrived at the Von Macht residence, the first thing we noticed were two policemen on guard by the stoop.

"Sir," I whispered, "maybe you shouldn't go in."

"Nonsense!" said Mr. Middleditch. "It has nothing to do with us."

But as we made for the stoop, one of the policemen hailed us. "Hold on, sir." He took a pad of paper from his pocket along with a pencil stub. "Name, sir?"

"Enoch Middleditch."

"Place of residence?"

"Forty Charlton Street."

The policeman wrote this down. "And your business here?" he asked.

"Photographer. The Von Machts are expecting me. What is all this about?"

"I'm not at liberty to divulge, sir. You may pass." They didn't question me. But I was sure I could guess what was afoot.

Pegg, as always, let us in.

By this time I counted Pegg as my true friend and trusted her completely. That said, I had not known her for so long as to be able to fully read her expressions. When she opened the door, she gazed upon me with such intensity that all I could guess was that her look was a warning.

As we walked in, I glanced at the stairwell. Scorch marks streaked the wall.

Mr. Middleditch, of course, was oblivious of what passed between Pegg and me, or anything else, for that matter. But when Pegg opened the door to the parlor, we saw not just Mrs. Von Macht and her husband, but another gentleman as well. The moment we appeared, I sensed great tension in the room. As it was, our entry was followed by an awkward silence.

Nonetheless, Mr. Middleditch went forward and made his little bow. "Mrs. Von Macht. Mr. Von Macht, sir . . ."

Witnessing everything from behind, I glanced at the writing desk. That candlestick was gone. But Eleanora's face was among the palms, her look one of mockery. I had almost expected to see her. I was sorely tempted to speak out, but who would have believed me? Instead, I tried to give no reaction, and just averted my glance.

Mrs. Von Macht was sitting on the sofa, hands clasped tightly before her, mouth rigid, eyes staring vacantly. On earlier occasions her hair had been perfectly combed and brushed. It now appeared quite untidy.

As for Mr. Von Macht, I had met the man twice, and both times there had been nothing but aggression in his demeanor. Now he appeared very pale, and whereas his hands had been like hammers, I thought I detected a slight tremor. In short, he appeared shaken.

Mr. Middleditch spoke up with his normal bravado. "Well, then, good day!" he called. "I trust I find you all well. Shall we proceed with the photograph session? I'll have my boy here bring in the camera."

"One moment," said Mr. Von Macht. "There are some matters to which we must attend." He gestured toward the other gentleman in the room. "This," he said, "is Captain Fogerty of the City Police Detective Corps."

Mr. Fogerty was a short, slim fellow, with a large, beaklike nose, a slack mouth showing small teeth, and frilly side whiskers—rather weasel-like, I thought.

"Pleased to meet you," said Mr. Middleditch. I could see he had become alarmed, though he struggled to hide it.

"Mr. Middleditch," Mr. Von Macht went on, "since we last met, we have suffered a considerable loss."

"I am so very sorry to hear it."

"Last night one of my businesses was destroyed by fire."

"Dreadful!"

"Arson," proclaimed Mr. Fogerty, and the penetrating gaze he bestowed on Mr. Middleditch suggested he was making a connection.

"I can only hope," said Mr. Middleditch, beads of sweat forming at his temple, "the criminal will soon be apprehended and brought to justice."

Silence filled the room.

I looked toward Mrs. Von Macht, who had yet to say a word. A tiny tic fluttered upon her cheek. Her right hand clenched and unclenched. I believe I saw traces of gray in her hair where I hadn't seen it before.

"Mr. Middleditch," Mr. Von Macht announced, "we shall not go forward with another photograph."

"How unfortunate," said Mr. Middleditch. "I was so much—"

"Your picture was a fraud," snapped Mr. Von Macht.

"Sir?"

Mr. Von Macht turned and brought Mr. Fogerty forward. The police officer cleared his throat and then, in a surprisingly high-pitched voice, said, "Mr. Middleditch, sir. A photograph of a ghost, a ghost which is presumed to be Mr. and Mrs. Von Macht's late, beloved daughter is, on the face of it, preposterous."

"But—"

"Sir," said the officer, "you will pay heed. No recognized scientific examination will allow for such a thing as ghosts, surely not a photograph of one. Ghosts are nonsense. Ergo, your photograph is a fraud, a swindle. It will not stand, sir. No sir, it will not. I am, as an officer of the law, considering swearing out an arrest warrant against you."

"I want to know where you got the picture of Eleanora," put in Mr. Von Macht. "That laughing image."

Mr. Middleditch's face turned quite pink. "Sir," he said, addressing only the policeman, "I must reject your . . . insinuation," he stammered. "Completely! If . . . if the Von Machts do not wish to proceed—"

"Furthermore," Mr. Fogerty interrupted, "you, Mr. Middleditch, are herewith requested—ordered—to bring any and all negative images that you may have produced of Mrs. Von Macht to me for my examination. Failure to do so shall ensure that I shall seek a warrant for them. And as you can see, sir, while I may not be a professional photographer, I know enough of the photographic process to determine if you have made a double image."

Mr. Middleditch, for once, was flummoxed.

"I don't know," pressed the inspector, "if you have anything to do with the arson committed upon Mr. Von Macht's property—or the attempted arson in this house or the theft of a silver candlestick—but the circumstances are most suspicious."

"What . . . what possible connection could any of that have with . . . me?" cried Mr. Middleditch.

"We are searching for one," said Mr. Fogerty.

"Sir—"

"Mr. Middleditch!" shouted Mr. Von Macht. "You are dismissed!"

"But you must bring those negatives to me," added the police inspector. "And be advised I know where you reside."

At that point Mr. Middleditch, his face now quite flushed, turned about and simply marched out of the room. A moment later I heard the front door slam.

I was so taken aback by what was happening, I remained where I was.

"I think that's the last we'll see of that fiddle," said Mr. Von Macht.

Mrs. Von Macht had yet to say one word.

Then, realizing I had remained in the room, Mr. Von Macht barked, "You, boy! Are there things belonging to Mr. Middleditch in the scullery?"

"Yes, sir."

"Remove them, and get out of here."

I glanced at the place where I had seen Eleanora's face. She was there—as I knew she would be—laughing silently.

"Do as you're told, boy!" cried Mr. Fogerty. "Before I choose to charge you, too!"

I bolted from the room. Behind me I could hear Mr. Von Macht say, "Pegg, go after him. Make sure he takes nothing that's not theirs and be certain he leaves the house promptly."

THIRTY-ONE

Pegg and I, not daring to speak, hurried down to the scullery. Only when we were inside the room with the door shut did we begin to speak in anxious whispers.

"They've suffered a terrible loss," she said.

"The fish-packing firm? F. Von Macht, Trader in Fish?"

She looked at me oddly. "How did you know about it?"

"I watched it burn," I said.

"They claim someone lit it."

"Pegg, it was—I'm certain of it—Eleanora."

For a moment she did not, could not, speak. Then: "What do you mean?"

"I . . . I saw her there."

"Are you sure?"

As I hurriedly packed our equipment, I told Pegg all that

had happened from the moment we parted in that room: my being unable to get out through the servant's door; seeing Eleanora's ghost in the hallway; watching her almost set the house on fire; what I saw at the burning of the warehouse.

"Mr. Von Macht was the principal owner," said Pegg. "He became so with Eleanora's money. And Horace, that candlestick is missing. They're searching for it."

"I think Eleanora used it to burn the warehouse. She used it to burn the stairwell. Was that noticed?"

"Of course. And that the front door was unlocked. That's why the police are here. They say someone came in—the same person who burned the warehouse."

"In a way, they're right," I said. "Eleanora is intent upon killing them."

Pegg shuddered visibly. She reached out and held my arm. Her eyes were full of tears. "Do you believe me when I say she used to be good?"

I nodded.

It took a moment for Pegg to compose herself. When she did, she said, "Mr. Von Macht thinks that your Mr. Middleditch is involved in some way."

"Why?"

"He must blame someone. Horace, they're both frightened, Mrs. Von Macht in particular. She doesn't grasp how, but she makes a connection with the photograph."

"I saw her in the room," I confessed.

"Who?"

"Eleanora."

"Last night, you mean?"

"No. Just now."

She stared at me.

Once I had gotten all our equipment together, Pegg had the carriage brought round. Then she helped me carry the things out to the street. We loaded the equipment under the scrutiny of the police.

"I forgot something," I called to the coachman, and turned to the house. Pegg came with me.

"What did you forget?" she whispered.

I waited until we were inside the vestibule. "Pegg, since I won't be able to come back, we must agree to meet somewhere and decide what to do."

"I can steal out at night. After they go to bed."

"Give a time and place," I said. "I'll be there."

She thought for a moment. "Tomorrow. Midnight. Union Square. The southwest corner."

"I'll wait till you come."

"Be patient," she added. "My time may not be exact."

"Pegg," I said, "you can trust me. I won't fail you."

With a sudden awareness of the dangerous situation, and with the shared sense of our frightful knowledge, we embraced like the friends we had become. Then we parted.

THIRTY-TWO

IT WAS LATE AFTERNOON when the carriage reached our rooms. I unloaded our equipment and brought it all inside. Mr. Middleditch was not there. I assumed he had gone off somewhere to sulk. Knowing the man, I had little doubt he was blaming someone else for his difficulties.

Prepared to wait, I spent my time putting things away and then did my normal chores. So it was only after some time had passed that I came across a note on my bed pillow that he had left for me, with a meager cash allowance:

> *Horace:*
>
> *I am off to Boston for a while. A particularly interesting engagement has been offered. Do take care of things. I shall keep you informed.*
>
> *Most Sincerely, MIDDLEDITCH*

After reading the note a few times, I had little doubt that Mr. Middleditch had taken flight. Whether he truly had gone to Boston, how long he might be gone, or when he would return, I could not begin to guess. Upon checking, I discovered that all his cameras were gone. No question then: He was escaping from the law, leaving me to deal with the consequences alone. How like the man.

I pondered what I should do. Since Mr. Middleditch clearly had no intention of complying with the police officer's demand that he bring all relevant negatives and prints to the police office, should I? I was sure my erstwhile master would be more than willing to let me take the blow that was aimed at him. Would I become implicated in his fraud? I recalled that the policeman at the Von Machts' house had taken down our Charlton Street address.

I studied one line in Mr. Middleditch's note: *Do take care of things*. Did he mean that I should destroy the evidence of what he had done? I had enough wits to suppose that might not be wise.

In the end I decided to collect all the negatives and prints that pertained to Eleanora and put them in my old chest, which was under my bed. The evidence would not be destroyed, but it would not likely be discovered.

When I threw back the lid of the chest, the first thing I saw was the Von Machts' candlestick.

Just to see it took my breath away.

I sat down on my bed and stared at it, trying to understand what it meant. I had no doubt how it came to be there: Eleanora's doing. That meant that not only did she know about me, she was more than capable of approaching me at will. She left it as a warning. A calling card, of sorts. It was one thing for me to know of the existence of a vicious ghost. Quite another for that ghost to know of my existence and where she could find me!

To say that I was very frightened is but the half of it.

But what could I do about it? I was not about to go to my parents' house. What could I possibly say to them? Could I talk about Mr. Middleditch's fraud, in which I took part? Tell them about the ghost? Say I was a seer? Would they not think me a lunatic? No, there was no way I could explain. Not to them. For that matter what could I explain to anyone except Pegg?

What I needed to do—must do—was meet with her. There was no one else from whom I could seek and receive understanding and help. Only together could we decide what to do, if there was anything to be done.

That meant I had more than twenty-four hours of waiting. With all that time before me, I went to bed, but not before I bolted the front door.

Somehow I managed to sleep, only to be awakened early the next morning by a hard knocking. My first thought was that it was the police.

I was afraid to move.

The knocking came again, more insistent.

I got up and made sure that the chest beneath my bed with the candlestick inside was closed and out of sight. I even looked about the house in search of incriminating evidence. None.

All the while the knocking persisted.

I went to the front door. Standing before it, trembling, I called, "Who is it?"

The voice that replied was low and tremulous. "Mrs. Von Macht."

THIRTY-THREE

I WAS SO SURPRISED, I simply opened the door. Mrs. Von Macht was alone.

How different she was compared to her first visit! Exceedingly nervous, continually biting her lip, eyes unable to focus. Her clothing seemed ill-fitting. Her hands clasped and unclasped. Her hair was in utter disarray. That hair, moreover, was now streaked with white. In short, all poise was gone while little more than panic and fear remained. She seemed anything but elegant to me now. And since I knew about her, and what she had done, my feeling was one of disgust.

I glanced beyond her. It was not even her carriage at the curb, but an ordinary, for-hire Hansom cab. Its driver was slumped over, as if asleep. Quite a contrast to her regular equipage. From all of this I presumed her husband did not know that she had come.

"May I enter?" she said.

I hesitated.

"I must speak to Mr. Middleditch," she said with some of her old authority.

"Madam, he's not here."

Her voice wavered. "Where is he?"

Mr. Middleditch, having unfairly left me to answer for his actions, I decided I would show the woman his note.

"Come in," I said.

She came forward and stood in the middle of the receiving room, looking about as if lost, as if trying to find her way. I fetched the note and gave it to her.

She read it, I think, several times. When she finally looked up, she whispered, "What does this mean?"

"Just as it says."

"Have you no idea when he will return?"

"No, madam."

"I'll pay you if you tell me. Where is he?"

"Madam, that note is all I know."

She crumpled the letter in her hand and then sat down, staring before her. Presently she looked up. "What is your name?"

"Horace Carpetine."

"What is your relation to Mr. Middleditch?"

"His apprentice."

"Then you must work closely with him."

"Yes, madam."

She withdrew again into agitated silence, glancing here and there, hands fluttering, tugging at her sleeves or bodice, trying to smooth down her hair.

I waited, now simply wishing she would leave.

"The photograph that Mr. Middleditch gave me," she said abruptly, "the one he took in my house. If I remember, you never said if you saw the image of my daughter in the picture. Did you see it?"

"I did."

"Did you believe it to be a . . . ghost?"

I could have answered in so many ways. In the end I spoke the truth as I understood it. "I do, madam."

"What makes you so sure?"

Once more I needed to make a decision. I suppose I had a vague notion that perhaps I could get her to atone for what she'd done. Or make some restitution to Pegg. "May I show you something?" I said.

"What is it?"

"Something . . . important."

She gazed at me. Then nodded.

I went back into the kitchen and pulled my chest out from under my bed. The candlestick lay there. For a brief moment I thought of bringing it to her, but realized that might put me in grave jeopardy. Instead, I took up one of the pictures I had taken at Green-Wood Cemetery—the one which contained an image of Eleanora—and brought it into the reception room and handed it to the woman.

She stared at it for a long time. At last, without looking up, she said, "Who took this?"

"I did, madam."

"When?"

"A few days ago."

"Why did you go to the cemetery?"

"Mr. Middleditch asked me to take some pictures of the Von Macht tomb."

She gazed at me, her eyes wide with great fright. "My husband says these are all trick photographs," she said with great anguish. "I must know the truth. I shan't punish you in any way. Is . . . is this picture . . . false . . . in any way?"

"What you see, madam, is a true photograph."

Her hand went to her mouth. She moaned softly. I heard her say, "Then she . . . has come back . . . to punish us."

It was not pity I felt, but revulsion. All the same I didn't wish to let the woman know how much I knew. She might guess from whom I had learned it. All I said, then, was, "Punish you?"

Mrs. Von Macht did not answer. She put her arms about her body with a slight twisting motion as if she were in anguish.

The room was terribly silent, though I could have sworn I heard that grandfather clock, the one in the Von Macht house, ticking. Perhaps it was my heart.

"I am sure of it," she said, and it took me a moment to realize she was answering my question.

Then she held out a trembling hand, by which I understood she needed help to rise. I gave it. She moved toward the door slowly, awkwardly, painfully, like an aged woman. I went outside with her.

At the carriage Mrs. Von Macht turned to me with fear-filled eyes. "She will kill me," she whispered, "just as I helped kill her."

Since the cab driver did not bother to help her get in, I did. Once she settled herself, I heard her murmur, "Thank you." To the driver she called, "Fifth Avenue."

The driver shook the reins, and the carriage lurched away, leaving me to stand on the curb watching. Just as the vehicle went round the corner, the driver turned back toward me. It was Eleanora, grinning hideously.

THIRTY-FOUR

WITH ELEANORA'S APPALLING IMAGE filling my mind, I returned in haste to our rooms, quickly bolted the doors, and dropped on the sofa, deeply shaken. Had I seen what I thought? Was that truly her?

I had no idea what I should do, or what my responsibility might be. Was it even my duty to protect this woman whose words—"I helped kill her"—amounted to a killer's confession? Should I let nature—fantastical nature, to be sure—take its murderous course by doing nothing?

No. What I felt was a compelling urge to help the living. Do not misunderstand. I did not wish to assist the Von Machts. Not in the least. Yet to me it seemed that to allow the vengeance of a ghost—even the ghost of a terribly wronged child—was contrary to the world as I understood it. How often I had heard my father say, *Let the dead bury the dead.* Did it not follow that the living should take care of the living?

Besides, wasn't it I who'd done the most to bring this ghost back into the world? Unintentionally to be sure, but it was my responsibility.

I took my cue from Pegg. Without having the slightest desire to provide a defense of the Von Machts, I wanted to find a way to put the ghost of Eleanora Von Macht to rest. Those had been Pegg's words. I wished to thwart the evil intentions of a ghost, no matter who her intended victims.

Then too, was not Pegg's life in equal danger? Had not Eleanora's ghost been willing to burn the house with her in it? So of course I wanted to protect her, very much more so than the Von Machts!

Finally—I'll not deny it—I wished to protect myself. Had not the ghost, by bringing that candlestick to me, made a clear threat upon my freedom? My life? For if the candlestick were to be found among my possessions, I certainly would be arrested.

The thought made me get up and slide the old chest out and open the lid.

The candlestick was gone.

Surely Eleanora had removed it. She had been in our rooms while I spoke to Mrs. Von Macht! Furthermore, since she had used the candlestick to burn down the warehouse, and had attempted the same with the house on Fifth Avenue, I could only believe she intended to use it again.

Knowing I must act, I locked up our rooms—as if that might keep Eleanora out!—and hurried to the Von Macht house. When, perhaps an hour later, I reached it, the first thing I saw were two city policemen posted at the door. As for any sign of life within the house, I detected none. Though it was still daylight, the curtains were drawn.

Gathering my courage, I went toward the main door. Past experience dictated it would be Pegg who responded to the bell summons. I never reached her. One of the policemen stepped before me.

"Yes, boy, what do you want?"

"Please, sir, I wish to see the Von Machts."

"They are not receiving anyone."

"It's of great importance, sir. Urgent."

"Didn't I just tell you, no one?"

"Could I just speak to their servant, Miss Pegg?"

"No one."

"But—"

"Be off with you!"

I remained there for a moment, trying to think of something that would gain me access to the house.

"But sir, I . . . I need to warn them. . . ."

"About what?" The policeman glared at me fiercely.

What could I say? That the ghost of an abused girl was

bent on vengeful murder? I would be treated with scorn, or worse, with suspicion. "Nothing," I murmured.

Frustrated to the extreme, I set off downtown toward home. Though my feelings of great urgency had increased, I could only put my hopes on my planned meeting with Pegg. That, however, was hours away.

As I walked on, I set myself the task of finding a way to get rid of the ghost. I reviewed all that had happened—particularly the way in which I'd brought Eleanora Von Macht back into this world. It was all through photography. Was there, I kept asking myself, some means of reversing the process? Was there something in photography, in *The Silver Sunbeam* textbook, that might provide an answer?

As it happened, when I reached Charlton Street and stepped into our forecourt, Pegg was waiting. She was standing forlornly by our door with every appearance of deep exhaustion. Gone were all signs of confidence; her proud spirit appeared to be quite crushed. At her feet was a battered carpet bag.

"I had nowhere else to go," she said tearfully.

"What happened?"

"All the servants were dismissed. The Von Machts plan to leave. They're trying to flee from Eleanora."

"When?"

"I suppose no later than tomorrow."

"Where will they go?"

"I don't know."

"You don't have to worry," I said. "You can stay here with me."

"What will Mr. Middleditch say?"

"He's gone."

"Gone?"

"Come inside and I'll tell you."

Once in our rooms, I got her to sit and made her some tea. Only then did I show her Mr. Middleditch's note. "So you see," I told her, "you're perfectly safe here with me."

"Why did he go?"

"I suppose he fears his hoax will bring about his arrest."

"But he'll return, won't he?"

"I don't think so. Not for a while. Not till this is done. He took his cameras. Even the spy one."

She relaxed visibly.

"Pegg," I asked, "did you know Mrs. Von Macht was here this morning?"

She shook her head. "All I know is that she went out earlier today and came back even more upset." I told Pegg about the visit, what the woman had said, and finally, that Eleanora had been the carriage driver.

"Do you think the Von Machts can escape?" I asked.

"I don't know."

"Pegg," I said, "if Eleanora intends to . . . kill them, it most likely will be tonight."

She nodded in agreement. "If they are there. Horace, Mrs. Von Macht is so terrified her hair has turned white."

I said, "Have you told the Von Machts anything?"

"I tried to. They won't listen to me."

"Would they listen to me?"

"No."

For a while we sat in silence. Then I said, "Pegg, do you want to prevent this thing from happening?"

"I think so."

"Why?"

As always, Pegg was thoughtful before she gave a response. "All I can think is that when you torment a person—and, Horace, they did torment Eleanora—the soul dies. When the soul dies, I suppose mercy dies too. Eleanora was good and kind. But all that remains of her is the torment. That's the part of Eleanora that's come back to seek revenge. Horace, I haven't lived very long, but I've seen too much death."

I reached out and wiped tears from her cheeks.

All I could think was, *I must do something—if only for Pegg's sake.*

THIRTY-FIVE

I FOUND BREAD AND CHEESE to eat and then made the weary Pegg rest in Mr. Middleditch's bed. While she did, I gave myself over again to trying to find a way to deal with Eleanora's ghost. Never was my sense of urgency greater.

I paced restlessly for two hours, trying to find some plan that might work. To no avail. At best, I was reduced to my earlier thought: It was with photography that I had brought the ghost into life, so might there not be something in the same process that could reverse the thing?

Desperate, I returned to the *The Silver Sunbeam* and kept skimming through its three hundred and forty-nine pages. I found nothing.

I was reduced to staring at the title page, as if I might see through the text and thereby uncover some answer. Then my eyes fastened on the words at the bottom of that page:

And God said, let there be light: and there was light

Call it inspiration, call it a gift from the divine, call it anything you wish: That phrase provided me with a clue, an
idea—a possible means of ridding the world of Eleanora Von
Macht's ghost!

Leaving Pegg to sleep, I spent an hour thinking through
my notion, trying to imagine how I could put it into effect.
I also went into our studio and checked to see if the materials I needed were at hand. Only when I was satisfied that
everything required was within reach did I wake Pegg.

She was refreshed but hungry. I rummaged for what food
we had: oatmeal, apples, bacon, and bread, enough to satisfy
us. While we ate, I kept myself from telling her my idea. I
wanted her to be fully alert, intent on my words.

As the hour was growing late, and time pressed, I finally
said, "Pegg, I think I may have a way of dealing with the
ghost."

A mixture of doubt and hope played on her face. "How?"
she asked.

"'And God said, let there be light, and there was light.'"

"The Bible. Genesis. But why quote it?"

"Pegg," I began, "the way Eleanora came back—the way I
brought her back—was so like a photograph. It's almost as if

she *is* a photograph. Remember, the more pictures I took, the more she came into focus, until she became real."

"But we need to make her . . . go away," said Pegg.

"Exactly so," I agreed. "My idea is to reverse the process. So that she becomes nothing again."

She offered a look of puzzlement.

"Pegg, do you remember when you watched me in the scullery? I showed you how, when you prepare a photograph, you treat the glass plates with a bath of nitrate of silver. When that nitrate of silver is exposed to light, the image is captured. Then, when I put the image into the developer—pyrogallic acid and silver iodide—the image appears. That's the way Eleanora's ghost came to be. But if you keep the image in that acid and iodide solution for too long, do you know what happens?"

She shook her head.

"The image disappears."

"Forever?"

I nodded. "Listen, Pegg. I believe the ghost is attracted by light. Wasn't it light that brought her forth? It's fire she's using for her vengeance. Well, if we could soak Eleanora's ghost with the developing solution . . . if we had enough light, perhaps we could . . ." I faltered. My idea now seemed so improbable, even to me, I was embarrassed to say it.

"Could what?" said Pegg.

"Like an over-exposed photograph—make her vanish."

Pegg stared at me.

"I can't promise it will work," I hastened to admit. "But I can't think of any other way."

"Where would we do it?"

"Where she'll most likely be. At the Von Machts' house. She's in pursuit of them, isn't she?"

"But . . . when?"

"It has to be now," I insisted.

She said nothing.

"Pegg, can you think of a way to get into the house?"

"The doors will be locked. But behind the house there's an alley. Back there, at the base of the house, is a coal chute. It has an opening. We might get in that way. I don't know if it's locked or not. I've never checked. Coal was Cook's task."

"It's already night," I said. "If we're going to do anything, we have to act right away. Are you willing to try?"

She considered me solemnly, and nodded.

THIRTY-SIX

First we needed to mix up the developer solution. As I put it together, Pegg looked on. If she doubted my idea, she said nothing.

I poured the chemicals into a large flask. These special flasks, as you may recall, were painted black to keep out the light. When filled, the flask proved very heavy. The notion of carrying it all the way uptown seemed daunting. And if it broke, all was lost. So I took all the money that remained in my chest, and leaving Pegg to wait in front of the house, went around the corner to Hudson Street and hailed a horse cab.

It must have been close to ten o'clock in the evening when the cab let us off at the corner of Fifth Avenue and Twenty-seventh Street. There was little traffic. Such light as there was came from windows and the few street lamps. No star or moonlight cut through the overcast sky. The air was damp and chilly. I found myself shivering from the cold and nervousness. And fear. The only sound came from an occasional wind flurry teasing dead leaves along the stone curbs, a sound that grated on my ears.

"I'd better check the house first," Pegg whispered.

She left me on the corner and went up the street to look. She returned quickly.

"I could see no lights on in the house," she said.

"Any policemen at the door?"

She shook her head. "And I tried both front doors. They were locked."

"What do you think?"

"The Von Machts have either gone or . . ."

"Or what?"

She did not say.

"Or what, Pegg?" I pushed.

"Or Eleanora already has"—she took a breath—"killed them."

"Pegg," I whispered, "would you rather not go on?"

"We have to try."

I said, "Lead the way."

Clutching the heavy bottle, I followed Pegg slowly and carefully.

Directly behind the line of elegant avenue houses was a

narrow, dirt-paved, dim alley. It was here that garbage was collected and coal delivered—as if such natural functions were best kept from the eyes of the wealthy world.

We went along this alley. I would have been hard put to find the right house, the buildings being not just lost in the night but very much alike. Pegg had no such problem.

"Here it is," she announced, all too quickly for me.

The Von Macht house loomed over us. Still, not a spark of light in any windows.

Having actually arrived at our destination, I faltered. But perhaps because Pegg was entering what was for her familiar territory, she became bolder. She felt about the boards. "Here's the coal door," she announced.

I crept closer and could see an indistinct square some three feet by three feet. It was not so much an entryway as a trapdoor.

"There's a lock on it," she said, giving it a rattle.

I set down my flask and took hold of it. It consisted of an old padlock with its shackle set through a hasp eye. I twisted it round. It gave somewhat, the screws or bolts that held the hasp to the door having worked loose in the old, pulpy wood around them. A few more vigorous twists and the lock fell to the ground. Though the noise made me wince, we were left alone.

Pegg pulled open the trapdoor. It fell out on rusty hinges. If it was dark outside, it was even darker within that square: absolute blackness.

"What's there?" I whispered.

Pegg knelt down and put her hands inside. She stuck her head in and then pulled it out.

"I think," she said, "I'm feeling a chute, for coal to slide down."

"How far does it go?" I asked.

"Don't know."

We held back for a few moments, uncertain what to do next. "Horace," she coaxed, "it's the only way."

"I know." I gripped the top edge of the open square, hoisted myself up, put my feet into the hole, and then sat on the bottom edge of the opening. From that perch I squirmed forward by kicking my feet. I felt the chute.

"Let me have the flask," I called.

Pegg handed it to me. I cradled it on my lap, holding it with one hand, then squirmed and hitched myself farther in. Balanced on the opening's edge, I wrapped my other arm protectively around the flask. Wiggling, I tried to inch forward.

My balance shifted abruptly and I dropped. Right away I hit the chute and, it being smooth from much use, slid quickly down. The ride down was short. Too short. When I suddenly hit the bottom, the flask popped out of my hand.

Frantic, I flung myself out and began to grope around what appeared to be a pile of coal. I found the flask, unbroken. The coal had cushioned its landing.

"Are you all right?" Pegg called.

"Fine. It's only a short drop."

Hearing her crawl in, I moved away.

"Coming!" she whispered, and in barely a moment, she stood safely by my side.

Though we could barely see each other, Pegg found a doorway at the far side of the coal room. She opened it with ease and we stepped into a hallway.

We were now in the house proper, as far as I could tell, in the lower hallway where the scullery and servants' door were located. For a moment we just stood, listening. The house was silent around us—except for the distant, infernal ticking of the grandfather clock above.

"Do you think anyone is in the house?" I whispered.

"I can't tell," Pegg said.

"Where do you think Eleanora might be?"

"She could be anywhere. You thought she would be attracted by light."

"I hope."

"We could light a fire in the parlor."

"Good idea."

I gripped my flask with one hand while holding on to Pegg with the other, and we made our way up the steps, with Pegg as guide. In the dark all our movements seemed magnified, so that our careful steps creaked and cracked and echoed around us.

We reached the main hall.

Whether I had become accustomed to the dark or whether the light came from some other source, I can't say. Despite the thick gloom I could see better now. The walls were vague and without substance, while the high ceilings faded into emptiness. The air was still. Carpeting muted our footsteps, though by contrast the ever-ticking clock seemed to have become the amplified heartbeat of the house.

As we moved down the hallway, I glanced up at the portrait of Eleanora.

"Look!" I gasped, pointing to the painting. The black mourning cloth had been ripped down, and the painting itself had been slashed in an X, so that the four canvas segments peeled back toward the corners.

Pegg stared at it.

"Would the Von Machts have done that?" I said.

"Eleanora" was all Pegg said.

"Why?"

"Perhaps she can't bear to see what she once was. Come," she said, and opened the front parlor door slowly.

I had been in this elegant room before, but it now appeared very different. There was a musty smell, and white cloth had been draped over every piece of furniture. The effect was to render all shapes glowingly indistinct, like a gathering of bulky white shadows, as if—it came to me with a start—we had entered the world of a negative photograph.

As I stood gazing about, Pegg dropped to her knees at the fireplace, piling coals atop wood kindling. In moments she was striking a match, producing a small fire. It was soon burning brightly.

Coming back to my senses, I looked about for candles, found some in the dining room, and brought them into the parlor. All was ready.

Side by side we sat down near the door. There was nothing to do but wait. We did not talk. We were too keen on listening; trying, I suppose, to anticipate all that might happen. The only sounds were that ticking clock and the occasional pop and snap of burning wood or coal.

Exactly how long we sat there I don't know. At one point I may have even dozed off. I was made alert by a sharp poke on my knee. "Horace," Pegg whispered, "someone is coming."

THIRTY-SEVEN

I JUMPED UP, GRABBED THE FLASK, scrambled to the other side, and frantically swiveled around on my knees and set the flask before me in easy reach. Pegg, meanwhile, shifted to a place close to the candles, matches in hand.

From outside the door I heard footsteps. Whoever it was did not enter. Instead, the sound halted just beyond the door, as if someone were hesitating. At last, the door began to open.

I gripped the flask and held my breath.

Very slowly, someone entered the room. I was already on my feet, ready to throw the liquid, when I saw just in time that it was Mrs. Von Macht who had come.

As though unaware of us, she stood at the threshold, her face turned toward the fireplace where the fire burned low.

In her hand was a small, lighted candle, which she held close to her body. The candlelight created what I thought was her shadow hovering high on the walls. Then I realized it was not her shadow; it was the sorrowful gray angel I'd seen at the cemetery. Her great wings were beating slowly. Her face, looking down, was full of grief.

I glanced at Pegg. Her eyes were on Mrs. Von Macht. I don't think she even saw the angel—nor could she.

Neither Pegg nor I dared move.

Mrs. Von Macht advanced farther into the room. She was completely altered, even from the pathetic creature I'd last seen in our rooms that morning.

It was not just that her clothing was all black. They were rumpled, not even fully buttoned. Disordered is the word. As for her hair, once so carefully groomed and black, it had turned completely white and dangled down her back in a tangle. Pale hair and skin framed eyes wide with terror. She continued to take no notice of Pegg and me.

Upon reaching the middle of the room, Mrs. Von Macht paused. She now lifted the candle and looked about, as if searching.

"Where are you?" she called, her voice low and raspy, almost a moan. "Why are you hiding from me?" The desperate and despairing sound of it sent a shudder down my spine.

"Please, Eleanora," Mrs. Von Macht pleaded, her head cocked slightly to one side, as if listening for a distant answer.

"Show yourself . . . to me." Each phrase was followed by a breathy pause.

"I know you're here, somewhere," she went on. "You're in the house, aren't you? I know you are. Are you near? You want to find me. I know you do. You wish to punish me for what I've done. Then come to me. I won't hurt you. Never again, my child. You have my word. I was wrong. Terribly wrong."

She sank to her knees in a pleading attitude, hands pressed together before her. "Show yourself to me, Eleanora. I'll restore your money. I'll be your servant. Your true mother. I'll beg your forgiveness. Please let me do so."

Above her, the gray angel loomed, wings beating slowly.

Then, even as Mrs. Von Macht continued to speak to the darkness, she crouched lower and lower until she was—the only word for it—cowering.

"Eleanora, I promise. Frederick shall never bother you again. I won't neglect you anymore. My place is with you. Eleanora, come to me and I'll beg your pardon. Ask your forgiveness. Just come to me, dear child."

Pegg and I exchanged looks over her head.

As far as I was concerned, the woman was completely mad, but surely no more than I—weren't we both summoning the spirits of the dead?

Now Pegg moved forward until she stood directly before the woman. Even so, Mrs. Von Macht gave no sign she recognized Pegg or was even aware the girl was standing there.

"Madam," said Pegg.

The woman sat up straight.

"Is that you, Eleanora? Are you speaking to me at last? I can't see you. Where are you? Show yourself to me!"

"It's me, Pegg."

"Eleanora? Tell me where you are. I'll come to you. I'll so gladly come to you." Her head was cocked to one side, as if listening. "Ah!" she cried. "I think I hear you. Is that you?"

She stood and began to move toward the door. Pegg stepped aside. Mrs. Von Macht passed right by her.

"Horace!" Pegg called across the room. "She'll lead us to Eleanora."

I heaved up the flask and we went out into the hallway.

THIRTY-EIGHT

Mrs. Von Macht was standing at the foot of the steps, holding the small lit candle before her. Near the high walls of the stairwell, the angel hovered, the beating of her wings in perfect rhythm with the grandfather clock.

Mrs. Von Macht gazed up expectantly. Her breathing was shallow yet agitated.

Pegg and I stood just outside the parlor door, watching.

"I know where you are," cried Mrs. Von Macht, and she began to climb the stairs. She went slowly, hesitating at almost every step, her free hand on the banister for balance, her head constantly shifting, as if listening for something. I had little doubt she was hearing something we could not.

Pegg and I followed silently.

Mrs. Von Macht, however, was still speaking, though her

words had grown indistinct. She certainly did not notice us.

Upon reaching the first landing, she paused. Suddenly she turned sharply and looked up. It was as if she had just heard something.

All three of us froze in our places. But then she continued up. So did we.

When Mrs. Von Macht reached the second floor, she went down the hall until she reached her huband's study. She opened the door and looked in brielfy. Then she continued on, going from room to room, peering into each one. Now and again I heard her indistinct mumbling.

As we followed, I glanced into Mr. Von Macht's study and gasped. On the floor lay Mr. Von Macht, dead.

I grabbed at Pegg and pointed.

Pegg leaned close and whispered, "Remember? She said, 'Frederick shall never bother you again.'"

I looked around. While we were staring at the body, the woman had gone up the last flight of steps to the third floor.

We gathered our wits and hurried after her.

Recall that on the top floor were four small rooms—the servants' rooms. The second room from the end was where Eleanora had died. I was certain now the ghost would be there.

Sure enough, Mrs. Von Macht passed down the hallway and opened that room's door. From within came flickering light.

Mrs. Von Macht entered.

Pegg and I drew in close behind her. I was still holding the flask, Pegg the matches.

Mrs. Von Macht was on her knees.

Against the back wall of the small room, standing before Mrs. Von Macht, was Eleanora in her black dress. She was holding the candlestick, its three candles aflame. The flames illuminated her frail face and body. Her body was mostly bones. Her face was exceedingly thin and pale, almost translucent. So was her long fair hair. Her mouth, which had been painted so delicately in the portrait in the hall below, was twisted, cruel, and full of anger. As for her eyes, they were large and clear, as though made of brittle glass, and full of sharp hatred, fixed on Mrs. Von Macht.

Eleanora in death was a perfect negative image of what she had been in life.

Behind and above her was the angel. A wind from the angel's slowly beating wings whipped Eleanora's dress and hair.

"Eleanora," I heard Mrs. Von Macht say, "I beg you! Forgive me."

It was then that Pegg darted forward. "Eleanora!" she cried. "It's me, Pegg! Dance with me again!"

A startled Eleanora looked away from Mrs. Von Macht toward Pegg. The instant she did, her face transformed. In place of fury there came a luminous look of love with such extraordinary tenderness as I had never seen before, all that Pegg had ever claimed for her.

Eleanora held out her free, transparent hand. "Sister . . . ," I heard her say.

It was then that Mrs. Von Macht also noticed Pegg. "Get out!" she screamed, and lunged so that Pegg was thrown against the wall. "Out!"

Eleanora whirled about. All her anger and rage returned. Leaning forward, she uttered one word: "Betrayer!" She lifted the candlestick high and took a step forward.

"Eleanora!" screamed Pegg. "Don't!"

But Eleanora's hand began to descend.

I leaped forward and splashed the developing solution from the flask on Eleanora. It soaked her face, her hair, and her dress. But taking no notice, she brought the candlestick down, striking Mrs. Von Macht a hard blow on the head.

Mrs. Von Macht moaned and collapsed. The candle in her hand fell away, as did the three candles from the candlestick. Rolling on the floor, they continued to burn.

With Eleanora lifting her arm, about to strike again, Pegg jumped forward and made an attempt to stop her. Eleanora easily threw Pegg off and advanced upon Mrs. Von Macht.

Flames spread across the dry old wooden floor and quickly climbed the walls. The tiny room bloomed with intense light.

Even as Eleanora was about to strike again, she began to

darken all over. Her very substance—if it could be called that—was darkening into shadow like a photograph left too long in developing solution.

As Pegg and I watched with horror and hope, Eleanora darkened to the point of disappearing until she became an empty void—a shadow that had no form—and then she was gone.

The solid candlestick clattered to the floor.

By then the room was almost engulfed in flames.

"Pegg!" I cried. "Help me with Mrs. Von Macht."

We tried to lift the woman. She groaned, so that we knew she was still alive, and we managed to pull her from the burning room.

Behind us the doorway was smoking, about to burst into flame. Very quickly the flames edged out of the room and like some living thing, began creeping across the hallway floor.

"Pegg," I shouted, "we need to get out!"

As I spoke, the adjacent room—Pegg's room—burst into roaring flames. The hallway was now filled with searing light, heat, and flame.

Lungs aching, almost blinded by the billowing smoke, I took Pegg's hand and started down the steps. Pegg hung back by Mrs. Von Macht's side. "Pegg!" I screamed, "Save yourself!" I reached out to her.

Taking my hand, she moved away.

The two of us all but tumbled down the steps to the second floor, then to the first and to the front door. The key was on the little side table. Pegg snatched it up and opened the door. A rush of wind swept in.

The flames above roared with renewed fury.

We raced down the stoop and onto the sidewalk, then ran down the street. Only when we reached the corner did we stop to look back. The top of the house, including the roof, was aflame.

I gasped: By the light of the flames, I saw the beautiful angel, directly above the house, rising ever higher on slowly beating wings. Her tears glistened like jewels. In her arms, held against her breast as if by a protective mother, was Eleanora.

Did I ask Pegg if she saw them? I knew she couldn't, so I said nothing. I just stared and thought . . . *Rest in peace.*

Within moments the avenue was crowded with onlookers. I could hear the clanging bells of approaching fire pumpers. Police began to appear. Hand in hand, Pegg and I fled.

THIRTY-NINE

WE RETURNED TO THE ROOMS on Charlton Street. There, behind a bolted door, we spent the rest of the night, and much of the following day. We were afraid to venture anywhere.

I was equally fearful that the police would come for us.

"We need to go to my parents' rooms," I told Pegg.

"But what will I do?" she asked.

"I promise my parents will be kind. There is only one thing," I said. "We can't tell them what happened. They'll never believe it—especially not my father."

"What will you say then?"

"I'll . . . invent something."

Which is exactly what I did. I told my parents a partial truth—that Mr. Middleditch had taken flight, fearing some entangling legal matters, that I was sure he was gone permanently, and that my apprenticeship with him was over.

I introduced Pegg to them and said she was an orphan. I told them the story of her early life and that she had become my dearest friend, but had been displaced by employers who had abandoned her most cruelly. To my gratitude my parents remained loyal to their principles and took Pegg in.

A few days later Pegg and I dared to go back to the house on Fifth Avenue. It was mostly gutted, its charred remains a monument to what had been destroyed. Seeing policemen there, we dared not approach too closely.

That part of my life was done.

But of course there was more. Much more.

Pegg and I stayed with my parents for some four years, until I came of age—at eighteen. I had found another position with a photographer and had advanced into becoming a professional. I focused on landscapes and works of still life, avoiding as much as I could taking pictures of people. Meanwhile, my mother shared her sewing skills with Pegg.

When I was eighteen, Pegg seventeen, there being no one else with whom we wished to share our hearts or our secrets, Pegg and I married. We moved from New York to Vermont, where I established myself as a photographer, she a fine seamstress. We had a child, a daughter.

We named her Eleanora.

From time to time when I was obliged to take portraits,

the images often contained ghostly figures—not always so, but all too often. In some cases I might manage to learn that they were relations who had passed on. I made sure not to take any more pictures of these people.

At times, however, I would see the sorrowful angel hovering in the background of my portraits. Inevitably the person in one of these photographs died within a short time.

I never shared these spirit images with my clients. By manipulating the photographs I could eradicate the ghosts completely so my clients never knew what hovered near.

Thus, no one else knew what I saw with my pictures—my spirit shadows—no one, that is, but my beloved Pegg. It's always been my solace to share my seeing with her.

But now—here is what I have come to. Our beloved daughter, *our* Eleanora, lies very ill upon her bed.

"Papa," she pleads, "take a photograph of me. You've never done so."

I make excuses. "When you are better. When you are healthier." But her illness makes her impatient.

"Do take the picture, Papa," she pleads. "If I were to die, then you and Mama would have something to remember me by."

I fear to do so. It is not the remembrance I fear. I fear that if I take my Eleanora's photograph, I'll reveal the image of that sorrowful angel. Or perhaps the ghost of her namesake, hovering close. Too close.

There is a limit to how much a seer wishes to see.

So here is my pledge: That I shall never take a photograph again. For though I am a seer of shadows, I wish to see no more of them.

Let these written words be a prayer that there be no more shadows. And may the hovering angel spare our Eleanora, that she might live well and long in the light of her parents' love—their bright love.

HORACE CARPETINE
Burlington, Vermont
1888—21 December